THE LAST MAN
on
Howling Head Island

A Novel

David A. Rhodes

MARGATE, NEW JERSEY

Copyright © 2015 by David A. Rhodes

All rights reserved. No part of this book may be used or reproduced in any manner, electronic or mechanical, including photocopying, recording or by any information storage and retrieval system, or otherwise, without written permission from the publisher.

Published by:
    ComteQ Publishing
    A division of ComteQ Communications, LLC
    101 N. Washington Ave. • Suite 1B
    Margate, New Jersey 08402
    609-487-9000 • Fax 609-487-9099
    Email: publisher@ComteQpublishing.com
    Website: www.ComteQpublishing.com

ISBN 978-1-341501-18-4

Book and cover design by Rob Huberman

Printed in the United States of America

After eighty two years of living by the coast of the Atlantic Ocean, I have written this fictional story.

I thank Judy Courter for her consistent encouragement to keep writing,

Scott and Victoria Becker for their technical and business advice,

and my wife Nancy for her constant patience.

Thank you all.

Contents

1. The Departure from the North 10
2. The Arrival at Howling Head Island 16
3 The Discovery of the Infant 20
4 John Kettle Speaks 24
5 Working at the Long Boat Inn 26
6 Escape from Hannah's Accident 29
7. The Abandoned Village 37
8. The Plague of Rats 41
9. The Raiding Party 48
10. Eleena Survives 54
11. The First Spring 59
12. The First Summer 63
13. The First Autumn 66
14. A Full House 69

Contents Cont'd

15. The New Arrival 76
16. Plans for the Hunt 78
17. Time Passes 80
18. The House of Thorns 81
19. Visiting Plans 87
20. The House at the Spring 89
21. The Nightmare 94
22. Bruce the Hunter 98
23. Alone Again, Disasters 103
24. The Wreck in the Dunes: *The Scorpion* 106
25. The Whirlpool 113
26. Whale Island 118
27. Hannah the Queen is Found 122
28. The Return to Howling Head 132
29. The Story of the Scorpions 136
30. A Message from my Father 137
31. A Final Departure 145

The Beginning

The sea, like a sleeping serpent, glistened in the morning sun. By noon the breeze had freshened, shattering the smooth surface of the sea into a million scaly fragments. As darkness fell the hungry sea began to hunt. The wind whipped the waves into a froth which blew high onto the shoreline. As the gale blew stronger in the blackness, there arose across the land the mournful sound of a howling dog which carried across the rocky island.

The Island of Howling Head arose from the sea, attached to the mainland by a flat salt marsh which often disappeared beneath the tidal flow at the peak of high tides, so that the grasses almost disappeared completely beneath the waves. The island arose on the ocean side to a ragged cliff from which one could look far out to sea. Just offshore of this jutting of the land was a smaller rocky islet which gave the island its name. The soft center of this offshore spire was hollowed out by the wind and waves, forming a cave with an entrance on the side facing the larger land mass. The Islet was separated from the main island by sharp rocks at low tide and a raging tidal flow at high tide.

The marsh joining the larger island to the mainland was crossed with tidal streams and bridged by a narrow road which led from the wooded mainland to the tiny island village of Howling Head. The name came from the sound which exceptionally strong winds brought forth from the hollow islet in the sea. Fierce gale winds blowing through the cavities brought forth sounds resembling the howling of dogs. It was a mournful cry heard throughout the island, and believed to be a harbinger of great danger.

The road to the mainland had a series of wooden bridges that crossed the winding tidal creeks of the marsh and then spanned the harbor to meet at the major building on the Island, The Long Boat Inn. The Inn had been built using stone from a nearby quarry. It was a favorite place of merriment for tourists who visited the remote settlement during the brief summer. The inn was called "Long Boat Inn" after the boat building industry of the earliest settlers, which was whaling. The rowed "long boats" were launched from the larger sailing ships to carry the harpoon crew to the prey. There were a few other permanent inhabitants who eked out a living from the sea or farmed the sheltered areas in the lee of the hilltop, and some retired visitors who appreciated the solitude of the island. There was a general store that carried hardware, fishing and hunting supplies, and building materials, a service station and a chapel which met the needs of the population, summer and winter.

Now, the island and the Long Boat Inn were almost abandoned. A small room had been built inside, on the dance floor where once merry music had been heard. The door to this small, cobweb filled cubicle was not locked. Two of the rooms' walls and its ceiling ended around the large stone fireplace which was built into one side of the main area of the Inn. Upon a tiny table in this sparsely furnished room was an open book. On the dusty first page of the book were scrawled these words:

"*I write these words for anyone to read. Do not fear for me, for I know the path well. The others have all gone before me. I am tired now and in need of rest. After all that has happened, I remain the last man on Howling Head Island.*"

My name is John Kettle, a name given to me by my grandparents.

Foreword

The inner room still existed. The door was closed but not locked, as if the occupant had only recently departed and was expected to return shortly.

When the door was opened and the resulting cloud of dust had settled, it could be seen that the small enclosure was dimly illuminated by daylight passing through two small windows, one on either side of the stone fireplace. The glass panes were frosted by exposure to years of wind-blown sand. The daylight was further dimmed by layers of cobwebs, clinging to every minute projection.

When the viewer's eyes adjusted to the gloom, the place had the appearance of a long-lost tomb. With closer inspection, the anonymous objects hanging along the walls, covered by a layer of dust, proved to be articles of clothing. Also hanging from pegs were tools for the gathering and preparation of food. In one corner were several long barreled guns. Scattered on the shelves was a collection of ammunition. The opening of the fireplace was partially bricked in, narrowed from each side, until it was just wide enough to hold a small cast iron wood stove, the firebox of the stove projecting into the room to keep the heat inside. The stove top had one opening for cooking. An empty pot sat upon this grate.

Chapter 1
The Departure from the North

It was sundown in late autumn on a cold northern shore. The young couple entered the doctor's office which was near the wharf. The last light of the shortened day streamed through the window of the door, its warmth giving lie to the chill in the air. The man's name was Jonathan Pesca, a marine scientist with his wife, Doria. The young woman was hugely pregnant. When the doctor had finished his examination, he spoke to them both, trying to convince them to reschedule their departure until their child was born.

"You are doing very well but you must realize how foolish it is to begin your journey now. Your child is due at any moment. Any excitement or physical stress may induce labor. In no way can I approve your plan to go on a sea voyage. You must not leave before the baby's birth."

The husband spoke. "I am sorry doctor, but we are leaving this frigid port tomorrow on the morning tide. I appreciate your concern, but my wife and I can stand no more of the cold. My contract with the oil industry has expired and I will find more meaningful employment in a warmer climate. If we stay until the child is born, and then stay longer until the baby is stronger, the harbor will be frozen solid again and we will be here until next spring. You are aware that we lost our only child accidently through the ice, our precious infant daughter, here in a previous winter. That memory has proven too much to bear." The woman, sobbing, with her face in her hands, nodded.

"We have sold most of our possessions and purchased the boat. All of our worldly goods are stowed on board and I have some money put away for a new life in a better place. When we arrive at our destination, wherever that may be, we will sell the boat and find a place to start our lives again."

"The boat is in poor condition, at best said the doctor. I have watched you load it, and you are not an experienced sailor. This is foolish of you both, my friends," the doctor pleaded.

"We are sure that the boat is safe enough for this trip. We may have scrimped on paint, but I know the boat is seaworthy," said the man. With luck, within five days, perhaps sooner, we can put in safely at the village on Howling Head Island. There is a warmer ocean current there, the harbor seldom freezes and there is a doctor, an old friend of mine, Dr. Brislow, who has an office there."

"I see that you are determined," the doctor sighed, "I will pray for you." The woman carefully arose from where she was seated. The couple left the office and walked slowly down the dark, frosty path to the pier where the old boat was waiting.

The frost covered deck was cluttered with boxes of household implements lashed to the deck by a maze of lines. The cabin was also filled with small household furnishings. The easiest access was to the bunks, where they slept in the wheelhouse under a wealth of blankets. In the first light of morning, they chugged out to sea, breaking the layer of crunching skim ice which had formed on the quiet harbor water overnight. Once past the jetty, they raised a sail and turned south on the shining sea.

On the first day, the sea, like a serpent, slept in the calm morning sun. On the fourth day it grew hungry and began to hunt.

The voyage southward along the coast was uneventful as the captain had anticipated. A warmer current weaved its way among the icy waves until one evening after dark, as they probed along the shoreline; they saw the faint glow of a blinking light, high on the top of the floating massive steel Bell Buoy that marked the entrance to the safe harbor behind Howling Head Island. The wind was blowing fiercely and directly into the harbor, while the ebbing tidal current flowed quickly in the opposite direction, flowing out and into the open sea. Huge, mountainous waves were driven without pause into the approach to safety in the sheltered waters behind the Howling Head Island.

The blinking light from the bell buoy flickered, signaling safety, ahead of the small boat. The buoy was partially hidden in the darkness by an approaching storm whose forked lightning branched out to all corners of the black sky, a vast webbed tree with many white hot branches. Suddenly, all of the small branches united into one mighty fork that struck on the booming bronze bell that was mounted on the top of the buoy, just below the light. There was a mighty "clang" that sent a burning shower of molten metal across the dark sky, hissing as it fell into the sea and onto the wet decks of the boat below. The sound of the damaged bell was changed forever.

The captain of the boat was blinded by the glare. The bells' warning tone, altered now from its booming sound, was now diminished by the lightning strike, the sound not carrying as far, but seeming to come from everywhere around him and the sodden deck of the boat. A huge wave from behind him picked the boat up and carried it toward the dark buoy directly over the wave ahead then fell into the trough below, almost invisible in the darkness. The captain was driven by the wind behind him, forced over the top of the wave ahead and then fell steeply down into the trough ahead. The man at the wheel failed in his to attempt to turn the boat away from where he thought the buoy was lying in wait in the darkness. Exhausted, he failed to steer correctly and his boat struck the buoy broadside. He was thrown overboard from his wheelhouse as the boat slammed into the barnacle covered buoy, crushing the boat's ribs and planking. Debris from the damage and the household goods stored on the deck floated away and were drawn beneath the surface of the sea, disappearing below the swirling waves and pulled into the tumultuous depths, and then driven toward the open sea. The condemned hull tilted again and filled rapidly, listing more and more, until green seawater reached the deck planking on the low side of the boat.

From below the deck, a young woman dressed in nightclothes appeared, crawling painfully slow and dragging a shiny, covered metal cooking pot at her side. She made her way down the slippery deck to the water's edge, leaving a bloody trail on the planking behind her. With each larger wave that washed the deck where she was lying, her thin night clothing swirled around her, moving with the water as though it was alive. She reached the edge of the deck and with all of her remaining strength slid the shiny kettle gently into the sea and watched as it floated away, high on the surface, catching the breeze and disappearing into the darkness toward the safe harbor behind Howling Head. The hull slowly began to capsize. The unconscious young woman slid down the wet deck and disappeared into the waves, followed soon after by the boat that had carried her.

In the darkness, above the sounds of the battle between the sea and the wind, came the sounds of wolf-like howling which gave the Island its name

Chapter 2
The Arrival at Howling Head Island

Howling Head Island had derived its name from the islet which rose from the sea on the ocean side at the far end of the larger island separated from the main island at low tide. The ragged shape of the islet resembled a canine head, tilted toward the sky, seeming to howl silently to the heavens. A jagged cleft at the sea level separated the upper jaw from the lower. A cave opened just above the normal high tide level. Worn by wind and waves, it marked the eye socket which became an entrance leading to a series of smaller caves and passages in the rock. It was said that in fierce storms, the wind blowing through these passages caused the head to produce the mournful canine sound, which could be heard across the main island. The volume of the sound was an indicator of the ferocity of the gale.

The islet itself was barely accessible, being buffeted on all three sides by breaking surf from the open ocean at time of high tide, and separated from the beach at low tide by a series of rocky pools which were interspersed with barnacle clad boulders. Only during half- tide on a calm day was the short journey possible, and even then it was only for the brave, the daring, or the foolish.

Once on the islet, a flat area below the eye socket provided a landing area where a small boat could be pulled to safety, and the adventuresome could explore the interior cavities, or clamber higher around the outside walls and watch for passing ships.

The main island of Howling Head was several miles long. The terrain rose from the lower southern tip, where the Long Boat Inn was built, to steep bluffs which overlooked the sea on the ocean side. The harbor entrance from the sea on the south end curved around this tip of land and the resulting calm waters were surrounded by flat marshes which separated the larger island from the mainland. From above, the land was tear-drop shaped. To the north, the highest point formed a blunted round mass overlooking the sea where tourists could watch for passing ships. The slender tail of the low southern section curled toward the mainland, and in that crescent shape was formed the harbor, sheltered from the prevailing winds by the northern headlands. The center of the island was dished out, like a shallow bowl, providing a fertile valley in which a variety of crops could be grown.

A freshwater stream, which began as a spring-fed pool in the highlands, meandered down two-thirds of land before entering the tidal waters of the harbor, flowing between small fields and groves of ancient trees. On the lower end of the island was an abandoned quarry which was used, for a fee, as a landfill by surrounding mainland communities, providing the few island dwellers with a small source of revenue.

A narrow road crossed the marshes and tidal streams between the mainland and the tip of the island. Low bridges, elevated on wooden pilings, carried the road across the winding tidal streams that crossed the flat marshes. Near where this road met the island, an inn, constructed mostly of quarry stone, had been built. This building, called "Long Boat Inn", was the social hub of Howling Head; boats being docked there at its wharf and the road leading away from the Inn going inland on the island for a short distance, carrying visitors and residents to the few shops and businesses that the island possessed.

Towards the islands' center, along the road leading away from the Inn there was a tiny nearby chapel, a general store which carried hardware, sporting goods and building material, a floral business that sold fruits and vegetables and a gasoline station. There were also several homes and a marina supply store which served the boating community. Scattered across the remainder of the land were small farms, fishing camps and a few summer cottages, including one belonging to a retired doctor, Dr. Brislow, who served as the local health center.

A narrow strip of beach ran from the parking lot of the inn, south around the tip of the island, out towards the sea. Accessible only on foot, it was a favorite walk for tourists from the Long Boat Inn. It included a rolling mass of huge sand dunes that were often restructured by the sea and waves, until sometimes the beaches going north disappeared entirely into a rocky jumble leading up to the islet which was the island's namesake.

Traveling along the shoreline away from the Inn, on the sheltered side of the island harbor, facing the distant mainland the rocks were interspersed by areas of salt marsh, shrubs and tiny, sandy beaches. It was a gentler shore, widening where the fresh water stream from the heights of the island met the harbor. Sometimes people in small boats from the mainland would anchor and fish in the sheltered water, seldom venturing out to the bell buoy and the open sea. The waterway which formed the harbor often flowed wide and deep before the salt marsh which began with several quiet pools on the mainland side. The marsh, in turn, extended to the tree line on the mainland several miles away. From the trees the mainland rose abruptly, echoing the rocky character of Howling Head Island.

Chapter 3
The Discovery of the Infant

On the island of Howling Head lived a middle aged couple who legend said were descendants of the original aboriginal inhabitants of the area. They lived in a small farmhouse built on the higher end of the island, near the beginning of the spring that was the start of the stream that led down to the harbor. They earned their living by farming, keeping an apple orchard, and selling their produce to the townspeople and tourists. When the farming season was done, the man and his wife would fish or hunt, or comb the coastline after storms for items which could be salvaged and sold to tourists or on the mainland. They were childless, which was a source of great sorrow to them, since they had no other relatives in the area and they were growing old. They were set apart from the other inhabitants of Howling Head, and did not mingle except when there was something to sell. The man was skilled in living frugally off the land and sea, knowing many secrets that he might have shared, but there was little interest in his ways. The old woman kept their house and garden secure and successful. The townspeople considered them strange and aloof because of their shyness. The fact that their house was the last house on the rough road discouraged casual visitors.

The one adjacent farm was inhabited by a young couple who used it as a summer home, and who became friendly with the older couple through the purchasing of fruits and vegetables from their farm. They had a newborn daughter, a tiny raven-haired child who they took everywhere with them. Her name was "Hannah."

The stream which flowed from the spring shared by the two homes was dammed in several places to provide pools of fresh water for irrigation and household use. This too was a common bond between the younger and the older couples. The stream meandered down to the bay, the narrow dirt road paralleling it, until shortly before it reached the salt water the gravel turned into a surface paved with crushed seashells, which lead into the business section of town.

Along the ocean beach front, there was much driftwood, weathered and convoluted, which could be gathered and sold to the tourist or the flower shops on the mainland. Sometimes, there were tangles of fishing gear; netting with floats and weights, strands of fishing line, sometimes with hooks, weights or lures attached. An occasional small boat or raft could be found, and if not too badly damaged, repaired and sold, or the brass fittings could be salvaged and sold as scrap. Once in a while a dead shark or sea mammal washed ashore, and the teeth could be extracted and sold to the curious.

One warmer morning, after the older couple had combed the sea front and gathered their prizes into caches which could be recovered later, they continued their day to search the back-bay shoreline. It was a gentler geography there with the land rising more gradually toward the higher lands. Small beaches existed between the shrubby plants and grasses that existed along the salty shore. The higher land rose more gently behind them now toward the sea side of the island. The beaches were short between the rocks and narrow between the edges of the bay and higher ground One day, as the old couple beachcombed after a storm, cradled against a rock and tangled in driftwood was a silvery pot, which had been carried ashore by the tide.

"How curious", said the woman as they approached the shiny pot "I can hear something alive and crying?"

She had straight black hair, streaked with gray. Her eyes were so dark as to appear black and were recessed deeply into their sockets. Her skin was brown and weather beaten from toil and exposure to the elements. Her husband, in agreement, clambered around the brush, and brought the stranded cooking pot down to his wife.

"It is alive," she said. "I can feel something moving inside of it." From within the pot came a cry that was barely audible. Opening the pot they found the tiny infant wrapped in rags and a fur coat of red fox fur, and the torn pages of an old family Christian bible. The pages were from the biblical Book of John, and had at one time borne a hand written inscription in the margins. Perhaps the mother of the newborn had left a message for the rescuers, but the dampness had caused the ink to bleed and run, until the words were no longer legible.

The child was cold. Instinctively the woman opened her own clothing and cradled the boy child against her own naked warm skin, pulling the cloth tightly around them. The man took off his own ragged coat and put it around her. They made their way home in great wonder, ignoring their other treasured findings and climbing as quickly as possible to their home.

The battered infant lingered on the edge of death for several days. It was only the tender care which was lavished upon him that kept him from sliding into the abyss of death. Eventually his labored breathing eased and he was able to drink a small amount of milk enriched with of butter and honey. They dare not ask for help for him, out of fear that he would be taken away from them.

"How shall we explain him?" asked the woman. "We will tell Dr. Brislow that we are raising him for his parents, distant relatives of mine who were killed in an accident ... he will help us" replied her husband. "We will raise him as though he is our own child. Do you have an idea of a name for him?"

'Yes," she spoke, "We should call him John," after the book of scripture which helped to protect him, and 'Kettle' after the object which carried him to safety. His parents would have liked that."

"That is a good name. We will teach him everything that we know, as we have been taught, so that we will be proud of him, and he will be proud of us," replied her husband, and so it was agreed.

Chapter 4
John Kettle Speaks

The book on the table in the room was left open to the first page and began:

My name is John Kettle and I live on Howling Head Island. I was raised by my grandparents who have lived here all of their lives. My grandparents told me that my parents were killed in an accident when I was very young, so I never knew them. My grandparents are very kind and wise. Grandfather has taught me everything about how to farm, and hunt and fish, and how to build things and repair any machinery. He can do almost anything. Grandmother taught me to read and write and do arithmetic. She is also very good at mending and making clothes. They are getting older now and they want me to get to know more about life away from their farm. They say that it is part of my education to learn more about the outside world and to mingle with the other people on our island.

I am quite content here, though. There are many things to do that interest me. I like to make things grow, and catch fish and hunt for birds and deer. My grandparents need my help. The summer visitors who vacation here seem strange and without purpose. My best friend lives near us in the summer. She is the same age as I am. Her name is Hannah. She has blue eyes and long black hair. She is the most beautiful girl I have ever known. I feel she is more to me than a friend but I don't know how to tell her that. Hannah and I grew up together, spending our summers exploring every part of the island, even more so when we were younger and

I wasn't old enough to help out with chores around the farm.

She went to school on the mainland each fall, and seemed more and more distant each year as her school finished in the spring and her family returned to summer on Howling Head. Only once could I dare her to travel to the offshore islet with me, using the old rowboat which I had hidden among the nearby rocks. We were almost stranded there one day when a large wave surprised us and threatened to carry my boat away before I had tied it securely to the rocks. She would not go again, but I made many more visits to the rocky caves by myself.

At the foot of a dense grove of trees, beside the stream, we shared our favorite private place. The wild grape vines had climbed onto the lower branches of the tallest tree, a cone shaped, spruce tree, and formed a canopy under which the vegetation in the shade had mostly died away, except for the ferns and mosses on the ground around the tree trunk, which could tolerate the shade. From around the lower trunk of this tree, by pruning away the dead branches that extended out from the l trunk, as high as we could reach, we formed a quiet hiding place where no one could find us. This secret place was such a favorite to us that eventually a faint footpath was worn into the ground. It lead away from the dirt road on the other bank of the stream and then across the stream to the other side and into our bower.

Grandfather has made arrangements for me to begin working at the inn on Saturday nights this summer, so that I can earn some money of my own. Hannah will be coming back to spend the summer. I can't wait to see her again.

Chapter 5
Working at the Long Boat Inn

Working at the Long Boat Inn was a disaster. After a brief tour of the kitchen I was assigned to the task of busboy, which meant clearing the tables of dirty dishes after the diners had departed, so that the table could be reset. The dining room was bustling on my first night. I was uncomfortable among so many noisy, crowded revelers, and performed my job awkwardly. The dishes kept sliding off my tray and crashing onto the floor. If the inn hadn't been so busy I'm sure that they would have replaced me and given me another job such as washing pots and pans in the kitchen.

At nine o'clock in the evening a noisy group of young people entered the dining room and were seated at a long table at the far end, near the kitchen door. They were in high spirits, obviously celebrating an exciting event. As I returned to the kitchen with a full tray, I saw Hannah seated at the center of the table dressed finer than I had ever seen her. She was stunningly beautiful! When she noticed me staring at her, she glanced up, at first not recognizing me in my sweaty apron, which was spattered with smears of food and grease. A glimmer or recognition flickered across her face, and then she gave me that breathtaking smile which I knew so well.

"John Kettle, how are you? It's so good to see you again. I have so much to tell you. How long have you been working here?" she continued, "But first I have the most wonderful news for you. I'm going to be married next week. "This is

William, my fiancé. William, this is my old friend and neighbor, John Kettle."

The slightly drunken young man stood up and reached out to shake my hand. Hannah did not notice the shock that the news had brought to me.

I was astounded, and did not extend my hand in return. He was immediately insulted.

"John Kettle," he growled. "Do you mean, Jack Pot or Crackpot?" Someone else in the group took up the chant.

"Jack Pot, Crack Pot!" They repeated the words over and over again, louder and louder. I turned, mortified, to flee into the kitchen but was bumped by a waiter coming out. The tray of dirty dishes that I was carrying fell onto the center of their table, spilling a mixture of food and drink into the laps of those seated there, splattering them with particles of gravy and uneaten food. William leaped from his chair and began pummeling me as though I had done the deed on purpose. I defended myself as best I could in this bewildering situation, but the other young men at the table joined ranks against me. Over the sounds of the scuffle I could hear Hannah's cry! Stop, Stop Now! The revelers continued, Jack Pot, Crack Pot! "Stop, please stop!" I was sorely battered, inside and out. I fought back, at first halfheartedly, not wanting to hurt Hannah's friends. It became obvious to me that in their drunkenness they had no such concern for me. In terror and rage, I finally screamed, "I'll kill you all, I'll kill you all!! Get away from me!" In utter frustration at this unhappy turn of events, I was overpowered, dragged to the door and shoved out into the dimly lit parking lot.

"You're fired!" were the last words I heard.

My grandparents were asleep by the time I walked home. I bathed my wounds and washed my filthy clothes, ashamed to let them see the stains and bruises. The next morning I explained that I did not want to continue working at the Inn, that it was too crowded and confining, and that I believed that I would be happier working in the fields or the bay. They must have known that there was more to it, for my face was badly bruised, but they said nothing, not even the following weekend when Hannah and William were married. I knew that they sensed my hurt but could not help me with it.

Chapter 6
Escape from Hannah's Accident

A year went by, a bleak time which was empty for me. I hardly noticed when summer ended and autumn began. There was no hope of seeing Hannah again. I busied myself with the operation of the farm, assuming more and more of the responsibilities. My grandparents were grateful but saddened by my own unhappiness. During a gale which occurred late in the harvest season, an old willow tree which stood on the bank of the stream near where Hannah and I often met was uprooted by the wind and toppled into the water. Debris carried by the current caught in the submerged limbs and formed a dam which threatened to flood the adjacent corn field.

Grandfather sharpened his two-sided ax until it was razor sharp and asked me to clear the stream. I walked to the clogged area early in the next morning. When I noticed that the willow tree had fallen at the place where Hannah and my own faint footpath had once begun I was overcome with longing for her. I glanced across the stream and saw the path, almost invisible now, overgrown, having been unused for so long. The top of the tall fir tree loomed up a hundred feet away.

By ten o'clock I had worked up a good sweat, even though I was standing in the stream. Warm sunlight filtered to the ground, driving away the chill. A flock of crows were noisily scavenging in the nearby corn field, part of which had been flattened by the same wind which had felled the willow tree.

The first hint that I had of not being alone was a soft singing voice and a rustling of the grass from the edge of the bank above my head. Pausing from my labor and looking up, I saw Hannah looking down at me. I was dumbfounded and almost speechless at such an unexpected pleasure. It seemed like years since I had seen her, and yet as though it was only a few months ago. She smiled her great smile at me, and instantly she was forgiven for the banquet fight at the Long Boat Inn. I was still smitten!

"I thought I heard someone working here. What are you doing?" she called. Her voice had not changed; still with the "little girl" innocence.

"What a treat to hear your voice and to see you again. I have missed you so much," I replied with a rush, for there was so much to say, and I feared she might disappear again as magically as she had appeared. I was ecstatic beyond belief, but afraid that this wonderful event would end with a blink of an eye, like waking from a dream.

"I'm sorry about that night at the inn," I said, wanting to get that apology out as soon as possible, for I had had no conversation with Hannah or her parents since that ugly scene.

"I know that you are. It was a bad evening. It was a good thing that no one was seriously hurt," she replied. She could not have known how deeply hurt I really was inside, even though there were no blood or bruises showing outside of me. She still had little idea of my affection for her.

"My parents are really afraid of you, for my sake," she continued. "You never should have said that you would kill us all. It was not like you. As long as I have known you I have never heard you say anything like that! " How could she have known how wounded I was at that time, with the announcement of her impending marriage? It was impossible to explain, even now.

"How is married life?" I asked, as casually as I could, though my voice broke before I completed the sentence. I cleared my throat, as though some physical problem affected my speech.

"It didn't work out," she answered. "William and I are separated, with no chance of reconciliation. He couldn't keep his attention away from other girls, so now he can have them, any or all, if they want him, because I don't."

"Father suggested that we come back to this island as one family again and see if we can be happy here together." The crows continued to bicker in the cornfield.

From the stream bank above, she called down to me, "Do you remember this pretty bell?" she asked as she touched the bell hanging from a leather thong around her neck.

"Of course," I smiled as I remembered the birthday present I had given her so long ago. The brightly polished bell gleamed like gold. I had found it washed up on the beach, among the rocks and shells. It was acorn shaped, slightly larger than an inch across, and held a brass ball which caused the bell to chime each time it moved.

"Is that the kerchief that I gave to you?" she asked, pointing to my red bandana.

"Yes, it is almost as good as new."

"May I borrow it?" I handed it to her and she made a parachute, a favorite pastime of ours when we were little. She fastened the bell to each of the four corners of the red square, carefully folded the cloth around the bell, and threw it into the air, as high as she could, where it opened and drifted gracefully on the breeze, down into the cornfield, watched by the crows. She enjoyed this amusement and I enjoyed watching her, leaving the razor sharp ax embedded in a log beneath the overhanging stream bank.

"It is so good to see you again. It has been such a long time. I'm sorry that I hurt you, and ask you to realize that I have been hurt too. My parents will be here shortly to pick me up and take me visiting on the mainland, but I wanted to speak with you alone for a few minutes."

She raised her arms to tie her hair behind her neck, widening her stance to brace herself on the bank just above my head. The sun streamed through the flimsy yellow dress that she was wearing and I could see that her figure was much more mature than I remembered from the days gone by. She was startlingly beautiful! My gaze was no longer innocent. I turned away and stared down at my muddy boots, lest she see the hungry look on my flushed face.

I went back to my work, wading to the other shore of the stream to drag some branches out of the water. Hannah, having thrown the parachute into the air, paused from her play, and standing on the edge of the bank above, called to me. "Father should be here soon. Please try to make peace with him." As she spoke, leaning toward me, she stepped slightly forward and the earth beneath her feet collapsed. Head first, she fell onto the gleaming ax waiting in the log and from there into the stream where she lay motionless, face down. The blood red water swirled away from her neck.

Fighting the moving water in the thigh-deep pool, I crossed as quickly as possible to help her, but it was too late. I could not stop the flow of blood from the terrifying wound. "Oh Hannah, my sweet Hannah!" I cradled her against my sweat-soaked shirt, kneeling on the stream bank, feeling her warm blood oozing through my fingers as I tried to stop it.

Her face, pale and serene, fell against my chest, as might a sleeping child's. Streaks of crimson trickled into the pool and drained away downstream. Hannah's yellow dress no longer glowed with the light of the morning sun, as it had only moments ago, but now took on the color of the shadowed water, streaked with her blood and clinging to her small, fragile form. I pulled her to me even more closely, hoping the warmth and life of my own body could somehow be transported to hers. The red fluids from the ax wound mingled with the sweat and tears which covered my clothing.

"Please speak to me," I pleaded.

I held my ear close to her mouth, straining to hear a word or a breath, anything, but there was nothing. I nuzzled her cheek with my own, as I had often longed to do. There was no response. Trembling with sorrow and fear, I carried her body to the leafy bower which we once happily shared and gently placed her body on the ground among the leaves .Returning to the site of her fall, I pondered my next move while attempting to wash away the blood stains from my hands and face. At any moment Hannah's father would arrive. What would I say?

From a distance high above came the ringing of the brass bell. A crow had carried it off and others in the flock were fighting over the gleaming metal and the trailing red bandana. As I watched, one flying crow carried it, red kerchief streaming behind it, to the top of the tree at whose base sweet Hannah lay. The cloth then tangled in some twigs, and the bell hung free. The crows, fighting with each other, were frustrated in an attempt to possess the bell and carry it away, pecking at it furiously, sending its ringing sound loud and clear across the field. I could hear someone coming up the road!

I had no time to think. I turned and ran in terror, leaving the bloody broadax wedged in the log. I ran like the wind, in panic and remorse. I fled to the rocky bluffs overlooking the islet. There, above the tide line, marked by a mark known only to me, was hidden the small boat and oars, which I dragged down to the edge of the water. I did not notice the condition of the sea, so great was my need to escape, though it was rougher now than for any other crossing that I had made before. Rowing furiously, I reached the flat rock below the eye socket of the islet. I pulled the boat upon it, and then up and into the eye, where I wedged the boat between two rocks on the otherwise flat floor there and fastened the anchor line to an outcropping...

The rising tide was already beginning to lap at the floor of the cave. I huddled in one corner of the cavity, trying to make sense of what had happened. The water continued to rise, and I climbed higher into the bowels of the rock. Darkness surrounded me as the rising water continued to pour into the cave through the entrance. The sound of the waves booming against the sea side of the islet reverberated through the interior of the cavern. I could feel the water rising, though I could not see it in the darkness. I continued to climb higher, pursued by the touch of the incoming cold sea, until, at last, my head touched against the hard ceiling and I could go no further. The water rose, first to my knees, then my waist, then my chest. I pressed my face upward and into a pocket of air, as the water reached my neck I clung to a rock which projected out of the wall, then became part of the darkness around me. How long I remained there, or why I didn't drown, I will never know. My little boat rose to the surface near me and I clambered aboard and laid down in it. Shortly after that the water continued to rise and my face began to press against the ceiling of the cave. I began to doubt that I would survive. In the complete darkness I lost consciousness, trying in terror not to rock the boat, less it tilt and fill with water.

Time passed! For how long I would never know! When I again became aware of my surroundings, I saw a dull light coming from below. The water was receding and the boat began to slowly descend to the cave floor. The light grew brighter as we neared the opening, less water blocking the light as the tide fell. The sea, still at an outside flood level, but below the entrance, was calm. It was morning, although of what day, I was unsure. It became clear to me now that I must go back to the island and explain what had happened, and in so doing, face the consequences, whether I was believed or not. The death of Hannah made all other matters of no concern. I launched the rowboat and returned to Howling Head Island. It was empty! No one remained!

While I was a prisoner of the sea, as I gasped for air in the cold darkness of the cavity in the Howling Head, an unknown catastrophe had swept across my world and driven away all of the human life that it could reach. The island was deserted. The world that I had known was empty, the island was deserted. The morning was clear and cool as I landed, and a gentle breeze rippled the beach grass. Other than the gurgling of the surf flowing among the rocks, there was not a sound to be heard; not a cricket, not a seagull, not a fish jumping. Pulling the boat back to its hiding place, I tied it to a rock and went inland.

Chapter 7
The Abandoned Village

I went first to my grandparent's house and finding no one there, I walked to Hannah's parent's house. There was no one there either. I made my way down the road, stopping with great trepidation at the place where Hannah's body had been. She was not there, which brought some relief to me in the knowledge that her body had been found and properly buried. I went from house to house, down to the great building of the Inn, itself. There was no one on the island. Looking out over the causeway which linked Howling Head to the mainland, I could see that the bridges had been washed out, swept away by the flood which had almost claimed me.

Most of the buildings were unlocked, as though the occupants had left in a great hurry. The contents appeared to be intact, as though there had been no time to save anything. There was no electricity. Opening some refrigerators and finding them near room temperature indicated to me that they had been without power for at least a couple of days. Since the electric transmission lines crossed the waters over the same missing bridges as the roadway, it was apparent that the power would not be soon restored. I began to empty the refrigerators of the rotting food. The freezer chests were better insulated, and I was able to salvage several meals before they spoiled. There were some propane stoves to cook with, and generous pantries of canned goods. Whenever I used anyone's supplies, I left a note listing that item, so that I could replace it when the right time came and survivors returned. I was determined to keep the property of the inhabitants of Howling Head intact, and thus partially atone for my part in the loss of Hannah.

There was one automobile in the bay of the garage repair station. The car had been partially disassembled, but the battery still showed some spark. Reconnecting the cables, I tried to listen to the radio but could find no broadcasts, only static. Thinking that perhaps that radio was defective, I searched through several houses for battery powered radios, and though I found several there were no stations broadcasting.

The first frosts came early. At first I tried living in my grandparent's house, but later decided to stay at the Inn because it was closer to the center of buildings and I could keep an eye on the town. In each house I drained the water systems so that no pipes would burst in the cold. I made lists of all the canned and bottled food in each place, and moved those items to the storage cellar of the Long Boat Inn where the temperature was more constant. I also was able to rig a hand pump there connected to the well at the Inn, so that I did have water for drinking and bathing. As it grew colder, I wore more and more clothing, finding that the large fireplace in the main room of the Inn consumed too much fuel and gave off little heat, which was quickly dissipated up the chimney of the huge room. I solved that problem by bringing in a small iron stove, and closing in much of the fireplace around it. Using building supplies carried from the hardware store, I built a tiny room within the larger main dance floor room, surrounding the fireplace. I built the room with two square sections, each section made up of a layer of wire cloth, over the wooden frame, and with a layer of insulation between wooden frames and then a final layer of wire cloth. The resulting sections were light enough in weight for me to handle alone, and, when put together around the stone hearth, gave me a rectangular room which was much easier to heat. It was illuminated by the light from the two small windows above the mantle on either side of the fireplace chimney, and light at night from a kerosene lantern. In one corner of the room, next to the fireplace and beneath a window where the first light of dawn entered the gloom, I built a small table to hold my book of daily writing.

A windowed door in one side of the dance floor overlooked the main entrance to the Inn, as well as the entrance to the basement storage room which was across the polished ceramic dance floor. My room was furnished with a water can, a bunk, a stool, a tiny table with my notebook, and built into the wall, a small cabinet in which was kept some canned food, knives and small tools and ammunition for the shotguns, ammunition and a rifle which stood in one corner. There were pegs at the ceiling level from which clothing and bedding were hung. Outside, in the main room, I kept a closed metal can for waste and I began to stack firewood inside and against the outside walls.

Before the ground was frozen too deeply, I gathered a plentiful supply of the root crops, such as potatoes, onions and carrots which were growing in the fields and gardens. I stored them in the cool cellar of the Inn where the more constant temperature would keep them for a long time. I buried other crops in deep trenches outside and covered them with hay, so that I could dig them up when, and if, needed.

The early winter was a busy one, and mercifully so. In the silence I could sometimes imagine the tinkling of the brass bell hanging high on the tree, and Hannah's laughter.

Chapter 8
The Plague of Rats

In the beginning of the winter, during a time when the ground was without a covering of snow, I went to the well supplied cellar of the Long Boat Inn to bring up some food for my meal. The trap door to this storage area was in another unheated room, so I put on my coat, lit the lantern and walked from my room.

As I stepped out, I saw a furtive movement near one of the stacks of firewood. Picking up a stick, I walked closer to investigate, and in the dim recesses between the logs, I saw a scrawny brown rat staring back at me. As I drew back the stick to kill it, the rat sensed my intentions, and rose defiantly on its hind legs, baring its teeth. It emitted a high-pitched squeal, even as I swung, and darted away, disappearing between the between the logs. The stick bounced harmlessly from the place which, a split second before, had held a rat. I could hear scurrying between the cordwood. It sounded like more than one rodent.

I made my way toward the cellar, cornering and killing one more rat on the way, and discovering another one on the top step of the stairway which led down into the cellar. It blinked once at the sudden burst of light from the lantern, bared its teeth, and leaped away into the darkness below. I had not been to the cellar for several days, and now was amazed at the damage which was being done to the stored food. Gathering as many intact roots as I could, and filling my pockets with cans of food, I swung the club and lantern in wide arcs which kept the rodents at bay.

I could *see* many pairs of eyes reflecting dimly in the glow of the lamp and hear the scurrying as they retreated away from me. I backed warily to the stairs, carrying only a small amount of food in my pockets since I needed one hand to hold the stick and the other to hold the light. Using my foot, I swept two rats from the stairs, one of them biting my shoe. I quickly climbed the stairs, slamming the trap door behind me. There were more rats in the main room, all staring at me with great interest, uncertain as to whether I represented a threat or a treat, their noses lifted high and twitching their bodies, ready to retreat.

Once within my sanctuary, I secured the door and took a quick inventory. There were several cans of water, a few potatoes and carrots, and some unmarked canned goods, the labels having been chewed away. There was kerosene for the lantern, six books of matches, but only a little firewood, since most of it was stacked outside. I would need to bring in more if I were to be under siege for any length of time.

Leaving the lantern behind, for it was still daylight and the main room was illuminated by several windows, I put on my heaviest clothes, boots and gloves, and, carrying a stick, moved out to the nearest pile of firewood. Tapping the pile sent several small beasts running, and by carefully kicking the individual logs I sent them rolling towards my door. In such a way I gathered enough wood for several days. Even as I brought the wood inside, there were several rodents watching me from the roof above my door, looking for access. There seemed to be even more activity around in the dim recesses of the main room. I could hear frustrated gnawing on the wire mesh above my head, and then from the floor level around my cubicle.

The Last Man On Howling Head Island

With the bridges to the mainland washed away, there was no fresh garbage from the mainland being trucked into the landfill. The multitude of rodents who lived there was starving now, and the aroma from even my small cooking fire must have drawn them to my lodgings at the Inn, where they desperately consumed anything edible. The ground outside was frozen solid and had locked in whatever forage that might have been available for them.

It grew dark, and I lit the lantern and fixed a small meal. Sleep was impossible with the sound of so many creatures climbing on and gnawing at my shelter. The scent of the food warming on the woodstove filled the room and permeated the walls, driving the rats into a frenzy, rattling on the wire walls, biting at each other with shrieks of pain, and falling from the roof with a thud. The walls held! I was thankful for the stone floor which they could not penetrate. The attack continued for two days and sleepless nights.

On the morning of the third day, I decided to counter attack. Taking a piece of wire mesh, I made a cylinder; long enough to hold a rat, but so narrow that the rat could not turn around in it. I flattened one side so that it would not roll when placed on the stone floor and sealed one end by bending it closed. Cutting a small hole in my wall at the floor level, I pressed the open end of the cylinder into the hole and baited the wire tube with a morsel of food. Instantly, a furry body filled the tube. I speared it with a sharpened stick through the mesh, killing it. Blocking off this opening to the outer room, I removed the body, and repeated the process, until I had a dozen scrawny carcasses. It had been a long time since I had eaten any meat, so I skinned each one and made a banquet meal on the wood stove. They would have made a meal of me if they were able to reach me.

In a land far to the north the snow was even deeper and the temperature even more bitter cold. Even the hungry snowy owls were driven south in search of food, their usual prey of lemmings hidden beneath the drifts, too deeply for even starving owls to find. Some of these birds found a temporary feast on Howling Head Island.

I heard a scratching sound from the small windows on either side of the fireplace chimney. Horrified, I looked through the snow-spattered glass as a pair of starving rodents, driven mad by the scent of food, gnawed at the wooden window frames, sending bits of wood and putty rattling down to the windowsill. I looked frantically for something to cover the window if they should manage to gain entrance, but found nothing. If the window glass fell out, not only would I be attacked by the hoard of small animals, but the bitter cold would turn my room to ice.

As I stood looking with fear at my windows there was an unexpected movement at the glass. Noiselessly, cushioned on wings that were designed to fly without a sound, a white owl, wings spread from corner to corner of the window frame, seized a rat in its talons and disappeared again into the night. Just as suddenly, another owl appeared and took a second animal, and then a third, until all outside activity at the window ceased and the only visible motion was the falling snow while the owls rested and digested their meal.

There must be very little food left for them to consume, I reasoned, and it is extremely cold outside of my room. If I cooked and stockpiled many rat carcasses, and kept warm by wearing as much clothing as possible, while letting the fire die down in the stove, maybe they would be forced to look elsewhere for shelter or perish of cold and hunger. It worked. I let the fire die down to barely a spark. On the morning of the fifth day there was no movement to be heard on the main floor around my room. When I ventured out onto the main floor there were no live animals, only the gnawed bones of those who had succumbed and were then devoured by the living. The storage cellar was empty of all vegetables, and the canned goods no longer had labels. There was an unusual thaw shortly afterward and I was able to go out to the fields and dig more fresh vegetables from the pits where I had buried them, this time hanging them from the ceiling beams of my room instead of placing them in the cellar storage bins. I also began to store seeds in glass containers, so that they were visible, dry and inaccessible without unscrewing the metal lids.

Suddenly I remembered warmly my friend the good Doctor Brislow. He had treated me and my grandparents many times during my childhood, and had taken a liking to me, suspecting something unusual about my sudden appearance as an infant on the island of Howling Head. I would do odd jobs for him and run errands, so we were comfortable with one another. One day he said to me, "I have a great gift for you. Any time that you are alone and in need of advice, feel free to visit my home, whether I am here or away. You may read my medical books and any records of treatment which I have advised for you or your grandparents. If all else fails and you still are troubled, go to my cellar and browse. Hidden there are secret cures for hidden maladies, some of which have few physical symptoms. I hope that this freedom of knowledge will be of use to you someday, even if I am gone."

I made my way down his narrow stairs, looking cautiously around the cellar which was illuminated only by a single cobweb covered window. At first I could see only the empty wine bottles which had been returned to the racks. Then there were small wooden chests of drawers, each drawer holding an array of small medical devices, though some held only scraps of paper with illegible handwriting.

There were dusty file cabinets with treatment records of people who had lived long ago, some on the island and some on the mainland. Nothing of importance was apparent.

The floor of the cellar was paved with individual ceramic tiles of many sizes, each carefully selected and fitted to its neighbor to cover a portion of the dirt floor from wall to wall. As I explored, one of the larger tiles moved beneath my feet. Getting down on my hands and knees I was able to pry the stone from its setting. In the dim cavity beneath the stone I found a badly tarnished silver serving tray. On the tray were three glass vials. Each contained a liquid of a different color. Instructions, written in Dr. Brislow's handwriting, were in a faded envelope on the tray. "There is a cushioned leather belt beneath the tray which you can wear and which will hold these vials and protect them against any damages. Wear the belt where ever you go and use the contents as prescribed for the following situations.

Red is for bravery. Take a sip when you feel that all is lost and you can't go any further.

Gold is for healing and restoration. Take a sip for illness, or use as an ointment to heal wounds or treat scars.

Blue is for strength. Use it when your own physical strength is not enough."

I wore the belt wherever I went from that day on.

Chapter 9
The Raiding Party

The weather turned colder again, forming thin sheets of ice in the harbor, which drifted in and out with the tide. Snow fell intermittently, until only the blackened flower blossoms of the chrysanthemums in the field that separated the "Long Boat Inn" from the chapel a block away showed above the drifts. The snow fell quietly, with little wind to drive it against my window panes. The silence was unbroken. How I would have loved to hear the sound of a human voices. I slept, and dreamed of Hannah's laughter, of my grandparent's patient instructions as a starving person dreams of food. I reflected on past conversations, imagining infinitely sweet variations. Gone were all the harsh words of anger or disapproval, only memories of kind and caring words remained. How sweet the world once was. If only for a minute I could return to the past and thereby change today. How lonely it is here. If only I could see and hear another person!

Sometime, during that snowy night, I awakened from restless sleep. Uncertain about the cause of my awakening, I lay in my bunk and stared around the room. There was a flickering red glow on the window panes. Listening, I could hear a noise which I could not readily identify. Was there also a human voice? Making my way to a window, I looked across the field. I saw crackling buildings burning furiously in the distance. The fires had begun in the furthest group of buildings that were visible from the window. Those distant buildings were engulfed in flames, the heated wood popping and crackling, throwing great showers of sparks into the night air. Close by, near the chapel across the field, three human figures moved deliberately around the building, and as I watched, a red glow began to show in its stained glass windows. I pulled on some warm clothes and draped a white cloth over me to break my outline in the falling snow.

Hastily taking a shotgun from the corner, I stuffed my pockets full of random shells and ran outside, hiding in the snow beneath an overgrown branch of holly hedge. The hedge, which marked the edge of the field, was unbroken, except at this place, which was the most direct path which the arsonists could use to reach the Inn. When they were certain that the fire in the chapel was well established, the three figures began to move in my direction across the stubbly field. In terror, I sat in waiting beneath the hedge, shotgun between my knees, draped in the white sheet.

I had loaded the shotgun gun in the darkness and in great haste. I had no way of knowing whether the shells were fine shot, such as might be used up close for rabbits or birds, or larger pellets such as might be used to kill a deer at a greater distance. I was in a dilemma. If I was shooting fine shot, I would have to wait until the targets were very close before firing lest I only wound them. I wanted, most of all, to call out and join them, to be part of a human group again, but there were three of them, and it was obvious to me they intended to destroy, loot or kill whatever or they encountered. They moved slowly across the field, closer and closer, toward me. The leader carried a torch on a long pole. The middle figure carried a can in each hand, while the third appeared larger than the others and seemed to be directing them.

I could not see whether he was armed because of the distance. There was too much space between them, so that as the torch-bearer approached my hiding place, the second person was lagging well behind, and the third was almost out of range, even of the heavier buckshot. As the torch-bearer approached me, the can carrier was still only a little closer than mid-field. The trailing assailant was so distant that, in order to be in range, even of heavier deer shot, the first person, soon nearing me, would be almost close enough for me to touch.

I waited, sweating even in the bitter cold and trembling with fearful excitement. Should I call out and offer to join them? Even now, joining living enemies might be preferable to solitude. On they plodded, bundled against the cold, their long shadows from the burning chapel behind them pointing my way. Wearily, the silhouettes approached. Puffs of vapor from their breaths disappeared quickly in the frigid night. I drew closer to the ground under the branches of the hedge, the white sheet hiding my outline. The falling snow reflected the color of the flames. Almost here! Almost here! I could hear the squeaking of the snow beneath their boots as they approached. Now! Without moving anything but my arms, I slowly brought the shotgun up and aimed at the center of the chest of the torchbearer.

"Stop," I shouted. I did not want to shoot, but was terribly afraid for myself, and infuriated over the destruction they had caused. At the sound of my voice, faster than I ever had imagined such a weary figure could move, the arm which held the torch drew it back as though to use it as a throwing spear. It flew in my direction. I fired twice. The gun belched a fiery orange blast of fire into the darkness and the body nearest me fell backward. The light and noise of the explosion from the shotgun momentarily took away my senses of sound and sight. When I could see again, the burning spear was impaled at an angle in a nearby snow drift. Motionless, I looked out across the field. I saw that the middle invader had also fallen, hit by pellets which had missed the closest raider. I aimed the gun at the third and furthest figure, which had broken into a clumsy run, impeded by the snow. The range was at a maximum, and had that person turned to run directly away from me, he might have escaped. Instead, the runner chose an escape route parallel to the hedge, unsure of where I was hidden. I fired three more quick shots, and the shadowy figure lurched to its knees but did not go down. The gun was empty. I fumbled desperately in my pocket for more ammunition, loading whatever I could find into the magazine. Two more shells finally knocked him flat. Now he was up and crawling away on all fours, screaming in fear and pain. I reloaded and fired again, watching the snow fly as the pellets raked the white field around him and tore into him. The agonized screams grew weaker.

    He struggled to his knees and turned to look for me. Still hidden under the hedge, I knew that he had not located my position. I put more shells into the shotgun and emptied the magazine at him again to stop the screaming. He finally fell, face down in the snow. When he was quiet, I too, lay down in the snow and retched, watching the motionless dark shapes in the pale field.

    There was no further movement from any others around the buildings. I had killed them all. When it began to grow light, at that mystical time of early dawn when all things appear magically indistinct I moved from the hedge to the nearest body and found it cold and stiff. He was a rough man, perhaps in his twenties, perforated with both birdshot and buckshot. I crossed the field to the furthest body, that of the would-be escapee who died such a difficult death.

Fearful and yet curious about the tremendous will to live exhibited by this huge man, I discovered he was armed with a pistol, and riddled with shot, and was also very, very dead.

Returning to the motionless figure lying prone in the snow in the center of the field, between the two dead raiders, I was astounded to find someone still alive! Curled in the snow was a young woman, a thin stream of blood from a head wound trickling down the side of her face and disappearing into the snow beneath her. She was breathing, though barely. I carried her to the Inn, laid her on my bed and put more wood on the fire. Boiling some water to wash her wounds, I looked at the damage which the shot had caused. At the hairline above her right temple a slug of buckshot had cut a three inch long furrow along her scalp. It was a bloody mess and might also have caused a concussion or a fractured skull. At best it was only a glancing pellet, one that did not penetrate or fracture her skull.

There was another wound which I only noticed later when I saw more blood on the bedclothes. She was wearing a heavy coat with large metal buttons. A stray ball had struck a button in her mid-section and been diverted into her rib cage, loosing much of its force at the damaged button. Nevertheless, it had lodged between two ribs, traveling under the skin away from the original puncture. I cut open the tunnel it had made, removed the deformed lead, and stitched it up with some fine fishing line which I boiled on the fire. It was a clumsy repair, but it helped to stop the bleeding. It was good that she was unconscious and could not feel the pain. She looked so pale, probably from loss of blood and overall fatigue. Her unkempt hair, curlier than mine, grew longer than shoulder length. I shaved away the side of her head that was injured, cleaning the wound as best I could and bandaged it, as Dr. Brislow had shown me how to do.

There being little more that I could do for the moment I returned to the chrysanthemum field and dragged the bodies of the dead to the side of the smoldering chapel. The heat of the fire had thawed the earth enough so that I was able to dig a shallow common grave for them, which I did. The next day, when the fire in the chapel was completely out I marked the grave with the soot-covered brass cross which once stood upon the altar.

Chapter 10
Eleena Survives

She remained unconscious for several days, partly from her wounds, loss of blood and partly from exhaustion. I bathed her wounds with snow, trying to reduce the swelling which disfigured her scalp. She slept peacefully, the slumber of the near-dead, barely shifting her position in the bed. Her skin was of an olive color despite the paleness of blood loss. Her ankles and wrists were thick and large boned. Her hands were calloused from the daily carrying of heavy burdens.

I returned to the room about noon on the third day of her recuperation, after a morning of cutting firewood and storing it in the main room. Having also snared a rabbit which I was going to cook for dinner, when I entered the room I could not find my skinning knife. The girl still seemed to be in a coma with no change in her position on the bed, but the knife was missing from the hook on the wall above her. The bandage on the wound in her rib-cage still oozed blood, and as I knelt to change the dressing, I saw a slight movement of her arm.

Bending over her, I touched the swollen area and saw that two of the stitches had pulled loose. There was an involuntary moan as I tried to tighten the clumsy knots. As I glanced into her face, I saw that she was watching me through half-opened eyes, and that she now held the knife a few inches from my face. Her fist was clenched on the handle of the knife, the muscles of her forearm were tense and ready to strike. I ignored her, and, as gently as I could, I washed away the fluids which bled from the ragged flesh. While I worked, she relaxed her hand and placed the blade beside her, moving her head from side to side in discomfort. I took the knife from her and hung it on the wall again, and changed the bandage on her scalp. The swelling had begun to go down. I offered her a drink of cold water.

"Thank you" she murmured. "My name is Eleena", and then she moaned and fell again into a feverish sleep. I was delighted to hear another's human voice, and in kind words. By first light of morning, I saw her stir again. I slept on the crowded floor on a small mattress which I carried from another room. "Water, more water, please," Eleena called. With some difficulty, she was able to sit up, propped partially against the wall. I put more wood into the stove, and soon had the stew pot simmering. The room filled with its aroma. Her eyes were more alert now. When I handed her my spoon and cup of stew she ate ravenously. When she had eaten all that she wanted, she spoke again.

"What is your name?" she asked.

"John Kettle." I replied.

"Why are you here, John Kettle?"

I explained that I had always lived here, and through some events which I did not understand, everyone else had left the island of Howling Head, and that I was its caretaker until they returned.

"They are probably not going to return," Eleena said to me. I was sent with the two men from the mainland to destroy whatever we found so that no one else could survive here and then to bring back anything of value that we could find and carry. We could see some of the buildings on this island from the mainland, and they appeared to be intact. There is no one nearby you on the mainland except scattered groups of people, each trying to dominate the other. It is a constant war to survive."

She continued, "I was selected for this dangerous raid because I did not bear a child for the leader of the group who possessed me. It was his belief that all women, upon reaching child bearing age, should have their first child fathered by him. "Why did you not have his child? It might have been so much easier for you," I asked. "The man is a tyrant and a greedy pig. His women mean nothing to him. He thinks that if he is the father of a large number of children of the tribe, they will be loyal to him. I had some pills hidden away. He had me many times, as many as he wanted, but I would never conceive, and so he banished me to this mid-winter raiding party, as a fuel carrier, as dangerous a mission as he could think of."

"Where are the other men?" she asked. "Dead, as I thought you were, and buried by the chapel" I said. "Where is the boat?" she asked. I replied, "The following day, after I had done all that I could for you I searched for it and found it hidden amid some heavy brush along the bank. I filled it with several open cases of liquor and many empty bottles that I carried from the bar.

When the Tide began to flow toward the mainland I partially flooded the boat it and sent it adrift with all of its contents. I hoped that whoever might find this drifting debris would believe that those aboard had accidently drowned while returning with their drunken loot. The water was full of drifting ice. Anyone falling into it would not survive for long. The fires here were still smoldering all through the day, so if their mission was to burn our buildings and return with things of value the mission may appear to have been accomplished, but with the fatal ending of a boat that capsized with the loss of all of the crew and salvaged goods. We may be safe from any other future raiders, at least for a while.

"It was a good idea to put the boat adrift. There may be more raids if some intact buildings are still visible. We didn't know our way around in the darkness. So there may be other buildings on the island that are still standing. If Moldono can see them from the mainland he may order another raid to finish the job."

"Moldono?" "He is the chief of the tribe who sent us," she answered. "If there are buildings still standing and visible, it is possible that we may have to find a way to hide them or carefully destroy them ourselves with as little evidence as possible. Only the buildings along the harbor heights are apparent from the mainland, and some of them are destroyed now," I replied. Perhaps we should find some black paint and paint those buildings that are in obvious view from the mainland as though they are badly damaged.

Among the buildings which remained intact were the general store, and the old doctor's home and office. The scattered homes provided a large assortment of clothes, bedding and furniture, while the farms, including my grandparents' provided various types of hand tools and tanks of kerosene and propane with which they were once heated. Many crops still remained in the fields and orchards.

There was one intact building which was particularly visible, having an observation deck that enabled the owner to look far out over the salt marsh to the mainland. On the next foggy morning I burned it to the ground, hoping that the fog would not lift until it was destroyed. I removed everything that might be of value, storing those things in a nearby unobtrusive storage shed. The mist remained all day long, and condensed that night into a light rain which extinguished the embers, so that by daybreak no evidence of the intact structure remained. Eleena continued to recover, and was soon helping me. We doubled the size of our room, using merchandise salvaged from the remains of the general store. We brought in new bedding which we placed against the wall of the new room.

Chapter 11
The First Spring

Slowly the winter ended. As it turned warmer, the green blades of new grass appeared almost hidden among the withered shreds of last year's growth. The buds on the fruit trees swelled and burst into blossom. The birds returned to fill the air with song...

On the mainland, as we daily watched, an occasional column of smoke rose ominously, but there was nothing seen close to our edge of the tree line, leading us to hope that our area was seen as having already been cleared, making future raiding parties unnecessary..

To be on the safe side, we decided to plant a number of small gardens in sites that would not be easily found, so that even if someone came ashore the island might still appear to be uninhabited. And so, in irregularly shaped plots, away from any paths or roadways, we grew small amounts of mixed vegetables, so that to a casual observer it might appear to be a group of wild plants. We found volunteer corn and squash plants which had sprouted from the seeds of last years' unharvested crops, and carefully nurtured the new growth.

When the fish returned in the spring we dammed the shallow mouth of the stream where it met the bay, forming a pond with rocks, leaving one opening where the fish could enter at high tide and then that opening could then be closed, trapping the fish inside. We netted the fish when the tide fell as they swam out of that narrow channel when we removed the stones that held the water in the pond. Undisturbed now, seabirds began to nest again on the marsh and rocky ledges overlooking the sea, providing us with a source of eggs and chicks in season. At low tide we waded out onto the shallow mud flats and gathered clams, mussels and oysters, storing any surplus in shallow tidal pools on the edges of the salt marsh.

Grandfather had a primitive device that he used to tell him the best time to begin planting crops which were sensitive to cold. This was a large flat stone high on the eastern sunrise side of the island. To make a calendar for spring planting, on the side of the flat stone which faced the rising sun was a mark which he had cut into the stone. On the opposite side, 180 degrees away, another mark. By placing a stone on the mark facing the rising sun, waiting for the rising sun shadow to fall, near or close to a stone on the opposite mark, he could tell the best time to begin spring planting. To plant too early was to risk the seed rotting in the cold ground, or of sprouting but being killed by frost. To plant too late meant that there might not be enough time for the crop to mature before it was killed by an early cold snap. He had instructed me in the use of this device, and it was a good thing, since I had lost all sense of time and only knew that it was growing warmer and the days were longer. We had no clocks.

Life was good. Eleena and I roamed the island in peaceful, if alert, harmony. Except for the loss of my grandparents, and the accident with Hannah, other memories of sadness were erased, and even those events began to fade, overshadowed by the business of staying alive. The probability of any friendly face returning to Howling Head became remote. Our conversation became focused on surviving as the masters of our island. With much joint effort, we were able to form two pools on the stream, one in the brackish waters near the harbor and one at a higher elevation where the water was fresh and cold. At the bottom of this latter pool, we stored some vegetables to keep them fresh. This pool we also used for ice in winter, cutting it into blocks and burying it in a large hole near the bank, covering it with a thick topping of straw. Thus insulated, it provided us with ice through much of the summer. In the lower tidal basin, we stored any surplus catch of fin and shellfish, the saltier water staying unfrozen longer than the fresh water pool above. We wove a net of copper wires salvaged from the burned-out buildings, and used this as a fence around a portion of the salty pool, to hold the catch that was stored there.

We inspected the clothing, cloth and bedding which remained intact in any of the buildings, and gathered it into the most secure room of each building, first selecting and laying aside any pieces needed for our immediate use. We did the same with tools and other items of hardware, particularly magnifying glasses, which we decided to use for the purpose of fire starting, saving our matches for those times when the sun was not shining. We always tried to keep some fire going in the stove, but, in spite of our best efforts, sometimes we could not rekindle the spark from the ashes. We also hoarded fish hooks, lines, and weights, storing them in several different places in case of fire or other calamities.

Ammunition for the guns was also gathered and stored. We seldom used these items because of the loud noise from the gunshots, preferring instead to trap our catch in snares or nets, against the day when these irreplaceable firearms might be needed for something more important than food gathering.

Chapter 12
The First summer

When the heat of summer arrived, we removed several sections of the portable walls of which our room was built. The heat from the cooking fire made the confining space unbearably warm. With the partitions removed, a slight circulation of air was possible under the shade of the high roof of the Inn. We walked the beaches in the cool morning air, as my grandparents had done, and searched for our own treasures in the flotsam and jetsam on the strand. Other than our own voices, we heard only the surf and the cries of the gulls which wheeled over our heads. I made a necklace for Eleena from a series of beautiful shells that washed ashore. When it was too warm, we swam in the salty waves and rinsed off later in the quiet stream.

The homes and buildings which were otherwise untouched by flames began to acquire an unkempt look, as the uncut grasses and shrubbery grew higher. The small garden plots, untended, except where Eleena and I had cultivated small portions, became overgrown with weeds. Vines began to overwhelm the fences, and extend themselves into the carefully landscaped trees around the buildings, or onto the sides of the houses, the tendrils fastening themselves to the siding of shingles, stone or clapboard. Along the path which led to the highlands the brush encroached from each side, narrowing the path even more, Clumps of grass began to sprout where feet and wheels once ground the life from new seedlings. In the untended fields, young trees began to grow, their seeds distributed by passing birds.

Honey bees swarmed throughout the thickets of wildflowers and into openings found between the walls of untended structures. The unpruned apple trees of the orchard bore smaller but more numerous fruit, bowing their weighty branches to the weedy ground beneath them. Creatures large and small have found an easy life on the island. The deer have found their way from the mainland.

Eleena is pregnant now, and we are ecstatic. Little shows of her earlier wounds, except for a small white scar on her scalp where the roots of her hair were damaged by the pellet that struck her. She has a raised welt across her ribs, but she is growing more beautiful each day and the gunshot marks are insignificant.

"When do you think our child will arrive," I asked when she told me the great news. "I think that it will be in late autumn, before cold weather" she answered. In the evenings we sat together and watched the fireflies appear, hovering over the lush fields. When it grew darker, the brilliant stars shone upon us. On certain nights, the full moon would ride at anchor in the black pool of the night. How wonderful life was.

We captured a newly hatched crow which had fallen from its nest and raised him as a pet, keeping the feathers of one wing, which was already damaged, trimmed. He never learned to fly long distances, but would hop along after us. Sometimes he would choose to ride on our shoulders, or if we were seated, clamber about our knees or even our heads, a source of great amusement.

We named him "Midnight" since he was almost invisible in the dark. At night he would climb, half hopping, half flying, into the rafters of the Long Boat Inn where he slept. In the morning, at first light, he would descend, and pester us until we arose and offered him some morsel of food.

    I went to Dr. Brislow's house, and poured over his books, looking for any information that would help us when the baby arrived. When the birth did occur, it was beautiful and without problems.

Chapter 13
The First Autumn

The air grew cooler and clearer. Looking across to the mainland, Eleena and I could see for a great distance across the tranquil waterways, and we detected no evidence of any other human beings. Great flocks of birds gathered together and wheeled across the sky with precision in preparation for the flight to warmer places. Along the oceanfront, schools of fish fed ravenously on smaller prey in the surf. The island teemed with life.

We gathered fruits and berries, cutting the apples into thin slices, and dried them in the sun. We brought in the products of our gardens and stored the surplus as best we could, in covered pits, cans, glass jars and in bins in the root cellar, some hanging by slender wires from ceiling beams. We were able, with some stings, to gather wild honey and stored it too, in jars, covering the tops with melted beeswax.

We caught fish and stored some alive in the holding pond. Others we cleaned and dried over small, hidden, smoky fires. Gradually we reassembled the walls of our room, and filled the dance floor around us with firewood. By first frost our pantries were full of foods, and we had no other needs...

One day, Midnight and I took a walk along the path of the stream. From the top of the tall tree which once held the hiding place of Hannah and I came the call of a wild crow, interested in the relationship between Midnight and a human being. Compelled then, by my own sense of nostalgia and curiosity, I went to investigate the old bower.

The leaves of honeysuckle and wild grape were withered, touched by frost, and falling, allowing great splotches of sunlight to penetrate the shade around the base of the massive trunk. The crow on the treetop flew off, circling us once in order to get a better look, and then departed. Looking up to the tree top, I could see no trace of the red kerchief. A few late-blooming honeysuckle blossoms cast their fragrance into the warm air, and I was drawn again into the past, and memories of Hannah. The dappled sunlight pierced the tent of vines, and reflected from a metallic object on the ground among the dead leaves. It was the brass bell, now tarnished by having lain for so long against the earth. A knot of red material clung to it. I shook it gently, hearing the musical sound which had remained unsung for a long time.

Midnight looked on with interest, turning his head comically from side to side. I tied the bell on a length of vine, and offered it to him. He examined it minutely, stabbing at it with his bill, and jumping back excitedly as it rang. I retrieved it from him, and put it in my pocket, polishing it against the cloth of my shirt as we returned home. The crow, tired of hopping, had fluttered to my shoulder. The bell gave a muffled tinkle with each step that I took.

From my travels on that day I salvaged several more kerosene lanterns and wicks. We also gathered more cans of kerosene, since the space we needed to illuminate was larger now... We were conservative in its use, since I didn't know how much more fuel I could locate. These things couldn't be replaced.

Early one morning, when the chilled world outside had changed to colors of brown and gray, our son was born.

Warmed by the glow from the fire, he nestled in his mother's arms, oblivious to the gathering winter. We named him "Hope" for that is what he was to us. And so, while snow drifts swirled about the Inn, and great gray owls hunted in the night, Hope pressed against his mother's breast and drew his nourishment from her. From the ceiling above his crib we suspended the newly-polished bell. When he was older he would laugh gleefully when it was rung, revolving on its tether, reflecting the lantern light into the dark shadows throughout the room. The days of winter passed almost unnoticed, such was our happiness together.

Chapter 14
A Full House

Time has passed. Hope has two younger brothers, Willy and Bruce, who is the baby of our family. We have enlarged our garden plots, having both the need and the helping hands to do it. We are content, but the boys are getting restless and curious about the distant mainland, from which we have seen nothing for several years. The island is becoming more overgrown. I have made one exploratory trip to the mainland after repairing an old rowboat and departing under cover of fog one morning five years ago. Launching the boat at the foot of the missing bridge near the Long Boat Inn, I followed the watercourses as they snaked across the marsh to their origins on the uplands of the mainland.

Forking several times, each branch became smaller and shallower than the previous one. Only the main stream reached into the tree line, the smallest end on the salt marsh at shallow ponds. The tidal water just inside the tree line formed a pond which was surrounded by a forest of tall trees line. The pond was lined by thick growths of the tall reeds which grew all around the water's edge. Among the reeds I discovered a hidden hunting lodge which consisted of one large room standing on pilings driven into the muck beneath the building. Hunters who used the pond tied their boats beneath the building. A ladder led up to a trap door in the middle of the building floor, allowing entrance to the cabin from below. A footbridge connected the shore to the house, leading to an open porch which ran around three sides of the structure.

The front of the building had no porch, but had two windows which overlooked the waterway which carried the hunters' home. Through these windows, the occupants of the house might watch for the return of the hunters. The building was intact, well-hidden and away from other structures which might have given a clue to its presence on the pond. I had intended to continue up the stream, hoping to salvage more copper wire or other hardware from damaged or abandoned buildings, but the tide had turned and was running out too swiftly for me to row against it. So, I returned to Howling Head along the same waterways, only now assisted by a falling tide.

As I passed over the remains of the missing bridges, I could see the remnants of the vehicles that had been on them when they had collapsed and been washed away. At first I could not make out what the rusting hulks were, as they were covered with barnacles, debris from parts of the destroyed roadway and sea grasses, and then were strewn in disarray across the bottom of the waterways. Some had been turned on their sides, and some overturned completely, some close and others having been carried away by strong currents. "Did anyone get off the island?" I wondered to myself. I returned to my family and said nothing about the wreckage that I had seen, explaining only that I had seen no danger, but that I needed to return again someday on the changing tide before I could complete my exploration.

They were intrigued by my description of the hunting lodge, and if conditions were different they would have built a similar structure on our own marshes. However, we were all acutely aware of the hazard of showing our presence on this offshore land, and could not permit any structures which might be seen from afar and which might alert people on the mainland to our presence on Howling Head.

I had promised Hope that when all of the chores were completed in the autumn following his fifteenth birthday, he and I would make a voyage to the mainland together, and I would show him the lodge. Willy and Bruce were very disappointed because they were not included, but they understood that the boat was small and that their mother needed their help. I also did not want to risk losing all of us at one time if any unforeseen event should occur. We started out before daylight at the change of the tide from ebb to full, planning to return on the same day or the next as the tide turned from full to ebb, always having the current helping us. We crossed above the first missing bridge in the half-light of dawn, the soft glow giving no indication of those sorrowful hulks which lay beneath the surface of the water. Hope would never know and I could only imagine the terror which had transpired on those bridges as they and the people on them were swept away.

Hope was a handsome, strong, young man, with his mother's dark hair that hung below his shoulders. In a carefully mended shirt, open at the neck, he plied the oars while I gave directions. When we reached the lodge and tied the boat beneath it, we took our extra supplies, two days' worth, up into the building.

Hope, who had been striving to prove his strength by rowing the entire distance, was exhausted. I suggested that he stay in the building while I continued to explore upstream, since the tide was still flooding in. "Stay here. I will be back when the tide turns. I don't want to be stranded upstream when the tide goes out, but if for some reason I do not return this afternoon stay inside the building and we will meet again tomorrow at the same time. Keep most of the food and water here, but give me some in case I am delayed," I instructed. "What if you do not return by tomorrow afternoon?" he asked anxiously, for he had never been alone before.

"Strike out on foot. Leave when the tide begins to fall, and is shallow enough for you to walk most of the way. Swim across the streams so that you can make it back to home before nightfall. Don't try sleeping out there on the marsh. Travel light, take a little food and water, and leave the rest here. You can swim across breaks in the road where the bridges were. Just stay away from the bridge debris, and don't let the current carry you too far if it's running strong," I cautioned. He looked at me anxiously. "Don't worry. If all goes well, I'll be back in a little while. In the meantime you might want to study how this place was built. Look around. Who knows what's hidden here that we might use on Howling Head. Take care, son."

The foot of the ramp which led from the balcony to the land was overgrown. There was no discernible path leading away from the ramp as it left the building, only a thicket of brush and greenbriers. Hope watched forlornly through the front windows as I rowed away. Rowing inland along the creek became more difficult than I had imagined. The water became so shallow and the stream so narrow that the oars touched land with each stroke. I beached the boat and proceeded on foot. The tide had fallen and I could see that I would not be able to move the boat until the water returned. I was glad that I had brought extra food, water and clothing. I had planned to spend the night huddled in the boat or hiding along the bank. The stream became a series of diminishing pools, as the stream traveled inland. As they aligned between the high gravel banks, the pools rose and fell in various depths and widths, trickling into one another when the tide was low, but when it was high, forming a continuous stream of brackish water which meandered through the forest. I continued upstream, hoping to find another building which contained useful goods, or to come across a path that might also lead to new discoveries.

Instead, I smelled smoke, as if from a fire of green wood. Leaving the stream bed, I crept carefully among the trees until I could see the embers of a fire glowing in the afternoon shadows. On a high bank which overlooked a pool, a flame burned slowly beneath the feet of a man who was suspended by his hands from an overhead tree limb. The man was bloody, as though he had been beaten. His head hung down, without movement or sound, as the smoldering fire burned his feet and legs.

In the center of the pool below, her feet tied together to a heavy rock and her hands tied behind her back, a young woman wept, tearful and cringing at the sight of the motionless figure on the bank above her. I did not know who else might be watching so I remained hidden. The girl was in no eminent danger while the man appeared to be beyond help

After sundown, moonlight pierced the shadowy darkness. The tide began to flow back into the pools, and I could see that the situation had been cruelly planned so that both the man and the woman might watch each other die. They had been left for dead on the previous high tide. But the young woman had managed to hold her face above the water enough times to gasp for air, so that though she was exhausted, she was still alive. As the tide moved up around her, forcing her to struggle once more to struggle to breath, it was apparent that she would not survive for another night. When the moon began to fall behind the trees, I slipped into the water. Keeping to the deepest shadows, I made my way along the shore as close to her as possible, and when the moon slipped behind a cloud, I half swam, half waded, to her and cut her loose, helping her to shelter on the bank a short distance downstream.

Taking part of her clothing and stuffing it with dry leaves and grass so that it might partially float, I returned to the center of the pool and attached this bundle to the severed line which remained anchored in the pool. Anyone glancing at this in the darkness would think that it was the drowned body of the intended victim, or so I hoped, and give us time to escape.

She was exhausted and trembling violently, and had not moved from the place where I had left her. We would both need to reenter the stream again, since we could not find our way between the trees in the darkness. The faint moonlight illuminated the stream like a path as I half carried, half-dragged, my helpless companion to the boat. Once she was safely aboard, I covered her with the dry clothing which I had brought along and began to pull the boat downstream stream against the current, the stream still being too narrow to row in, particularly in the dark. When we reached the lodge, we paused only long enough to exchange her wet clothing for dry, bundling her in several layers, before starting out again, taking everything with us so that there would be no evidence of our presence in the building. Hope's eyes were wide with excitement. He had never seen a woman other than his mother.

She huddled in the bow of the boat, saying nothing and trembling violently, even under all of the layers of clothing in which we wrapped her. I was not sure that she would be alive when we reached the safety of our home on Howling Head, but she was.

Chapter 15

The New Arrival

Eleena took our new guest to a place in front of the woodstove, and though the day was not cold, built a roaring fire so that her trembling might cease. She arranged a cot close to the fire where the pale and exhausted woman could rest.

After a warm meal, she recovered enough to recognize us as friends. We gathered around her, the boys all in wonder, for she was beautiful in spite of her battered appearance. Eleena explained to her that she, too, had once lived on the mainland and experienced harsh treatment at the hands of Moldono and his gang.

"I am called Rosanne. I have escaped from Moldono, or rather by your kindness, you have rescued me. He was trying to drown me because I am pregnant by another man with my first child. The father of my child was the dead man that you saw hanging by his hands over the fire. We were lovers. He would not lie even to Moldono. When he was asked if we were lovers, he told the truth and so we paid the price. He was a brave and gentle man."

"Moldono will pay," she continued." His children hate him. They see what privileges he demands for himself, and how they and their mothers live. They only wait for the right moment," she said, and then began to sob in great, uncontrollable spasms which shook the cot on which she rested. She turned her head away from us, as if she could not share her grief. Eleena covered her with one more blanket and we went into the main room to give her time to recover. We banked the fire for the night and slept around her. In the morning we decided to build a separate area on each side of our room, with a doorway leading to ours so that the heat would circulate. The three boys shared the larger of the new rooms, while pregnant Rosanne was given the privacy of the other.

She soon proved herself excellent with a needle and thread, and so assumed the responsibility of patching our clothes and piecing together cloth for our bedding. She was well suited for our domestic needs around the Inn. She began to show the child growing within her. When the birth occurred, it brought bring twin girls into our world. She named them "Aries" and "Aquarius" after the constellations which were visible in the night sky.

Chapter 16
Plans for the Hunt

The boys, Willy in particular, were involved in inventing devices which made our labor easier, first constructing a water wheel which powered a saw blade and a grindstone for shaping other stones and metals. In a book, they found some instructions for smelting metal, and built a crude furnace in a vertical fissure in the sea cliffs, pouring the molten metal, mostly salvaged copper, into clay molds.

Bruce was the hunting and fishing expert. There were, at certain times of the year, vast multitudes of waterfowl that plied the seas and marshes around our island. As they visited us each spring and fall, we found our way to capture as many as we needed, without depleting our limited supply of ammunition.

Knowing the areas of the waters where large concentrations of the waterfowl fed, Bruce cut some wooden blocks into the rough shapes of swimming birds, and charred them with fire until they were evenly dark colored, imitating the appearance of the live birds. Each decoy had two lines fastened to its bottom, and a weight which acted as ballast and kept it right-side-up in the water. One line was long enough to anchor the decoy to the shallow bottom of the pond, or to be tied to a stake on the bank. A second, shorter line was attached to each block, and on that line were baited fish hooks. The wild birds became attracted to the decoys, and, swimming around in their midst, became entangled in the baited lines. The first bird to become hooked would act as a lure for the others by dragging the decoy around the pond and giving it the semblance of being alive. More birds would be attracted. In this manner many birds could be brought to the table for immediate consumption, or stored on ice for future use. Occasionally, large schools of fish would also seize the baited hooks and present a mixed bag for the hunter-fisherman.

In trying to capture the deer which shared the island with us, I asked Willy to design a light weight cover for pits dug and hidden along the deer trails. The cover would have to be light enough to be easily carried, and able to be disguised with a covering of twigs and leaves. It would need to have a trigger mechanism that would allow the passage of small animals, rabbits, squirrels and birds without allowing the cover to fall into the pit, but would give way under a deer's weight. My plan was to dig a series of these pits along the deer trails, and by trapping them, insure us a constant supply of meat. Willy complied, but we, ourselves, had to be careful when walking in the woods and be aware of where the pits were dug. A small branch was added to the trail on either side of the pit so that instead of walking, the deer would jump over the branch and land on the disguised cover. It worked well, and we had a sufficient supply of venison without much effort.

Chapter 17
Time Passes

The island has continued to become more and more overgrown. The number of deer has decreased as the former fields in which they grazed have become overgrown and turned to thicker forests. We have abandoned the small, irregular garden plots, there seemingly being no need to fear another invasion. The fields are larger now, but not as large as they once were, since they must all be tended by hand labor.

We have plenty and are well fed. I regret that the island is returning to its wild condition, there not being enough foot traffic to keep the road and pathways open. The buildings away from the Long Boat Inn are in disrepair. Some have almost disappeared beneath cloaks of vines which have invaded even interior spaces through missing window panes. Plants grow in the clogged rain gutters which remain, many of them having filled with rotted rain-soaked leaves and fallen to the ground.

There is no way to tell· where lawns once began and the streets once edged, since both are now filled with undergrowth. Only the paths between our gardens and the ponds remain in regular use. The seacoast is always open to foot passage as are the marshes along the harbor. The beaches in particular are often scoured clean by the moving water.

Chapter 18
The House of Thorns

One day Hope came to me and said, "Father, I would like to start my own life. I'm old enough, and you have taught me how to survive and prosper. I need to make my own way."

I was caught unaware of his feelings. He was just a boy, and perhaps he always would be. "Where will you go; what will you do?" I asked, thinking that he would choose to live in one of the abandoned buildings of Howling Head. It would be good to have a reason to travel to another part of the island and keep the paths open.

"Do you remember the hunting lodge on the other side of the harbor? That's where I want to live. We need an outpost on the mainland. If there is a problem, I will know it first and warn you somehow."

"Won't you be lonely over there by yourself?" I argued, knowing how much we would miss him here, if he left.

"I will miss my family very much! Rosanne has said that she would like to go with me and bring the twins. She would like to have her own home, on the mainland."

"Isn't she afraid to go back?"

"Yes, but that is where she belongs. She is not an islander."

"How will you protect yourselves?" I questioned.

"By staying hidden as you do; clearing small areas for gardens, and foraging on the marsh. We can travel on the water instead of leaving trails on the land. We will have to build another boat, large enough to hold the four of us. Maybe when we are settled over there, I can build a smaller boat to scout in. It's not that far. Once we are over there, we can visit with you on a regular schedule. There must be things over there that you need, and we can certainly use the food that you gather from here," he presented his case.

"Have you mentioned it to your mother?"

"Not yet. I wanted to see what you would say first."

"Let's think about it. There are a lot of things to be considered." I was stalling. The idea of a family member living away from the island was so new that I had no firm reply.

"It is your life, and we have done the best that we can, and taught you everything that we know. You are young and strong and resourceful.

If it does work out, and that is where you choose to live, we will give you all the help that we can."

"I know that you will," said Hope.

"What supplies will you need to start with?"

"We will need food, and of course and seeds for spring planting. We will need enough clothes and bedding to keep warm and containers for storage. Also useful will be tools, axes and knives which Willy can make if you have none to spare. Of course we will need some way to start a fire for cooking and warmth. For protection we can use a gun and ammunition, but only if you can spare them,"

"How do you intend to make the house on stilts livable? How will you make it safer, if you can?"

"First father, it has a natural moat around it. If we disconnect the walkway that connects to the land, it will make it difficult for anyone to reach us. We can bar the door which comes in from below, so that intruders can't get in from that direction.

"Second, we can board up the porch, and use that as storage area. This will also give us some added insulation from the cold and heat."

"Third, the cabin is too visible from the stream. Some type of floating camouflaged baffle will have to be built and planted with high reeds, one that lets us get the boats in and out, yet doesn't allow a line-of-sight view of the building from the stream."

"Fourth," he continued, "I propose that we plant or transplant briars on all three land sides of the pool, as close together as we can get them to grow. We can girdle the trunks of larger trees which are already there and killing those trees whose foliage might cast too much shadow on the young briar plants. It will appear that the trees have died of natural causes, but the briars will climb into their lower branches and form a wall of thorns which no one will want to penetrate."

He had thought it out well.

"When do you propose to leave?" I asked this question with some concern, since I was afraid that he would wish to leave immediately. I had grown accustomed to the laughter of Aries and Aquarius and the sound of their feet running about the Inn. Gentle Rosanne, always busy with some home making task, using the last bit of light for one more stitch, was a vision that I had become used to.

"In two years we should be living there. That's how long it will take to make the changes, if we have the time to work on it."

He showed surprising maturity. That gradual grace period would allow his mother and me to grow accustomed to the idea that our first child was responsible enough to be on his own. I agreed to the scheme, and together Hope and I explained it to his mother. There was plenty of time to have a change of heart or to lengthen the departure date if that should be needed.

We began by girdling the trees, taking axes to the bark just above the ground line, and removing several inches of the bark and the sap-carrying tissue beneath it, so that no nutrients could reach the upper branches. We cut several of the trees completely down, felling them in such a way that they landed in the water, and we were able to half drag, half float them across the pond to make the baffle, positioning them in a way that made them appear to be a natural log jam..

With each voyage we brought with us the roots of briars, hacking a slot in the earth for each piece, dropping in the root, and tamping the trench closed with our feet. One of the chores of those who stayed on the island while Hope and I were reconstructing the lodge was to search out and dig the briars, keeping them packed in moist grass, until ready to be transplanted. Usually our boat was so filled with supplies that there was barely room for Hope and me.

All of the wood necessary to enclose the porch was salvaged from the unused buildings nearest the Inn on Howling Head, which was a task that was left to Willy and Bruce. Care had to be taken that the boards were not split or broken as they were removed, since we had no way to square them up, other than hand saws, once we were left the mainland. Salvaged nails were also at a premium, since those which held the planks on the exterior of the salvaged building were often too rusted for re-use. The finished enclosure, however, looked as weathered as the original building and functioned as had been hoped.

Bucketful by bucketful, we scooped out sand and muck from the basin around the lodge and poured it into the interior of the baffle, until the ground rose above the water. Upon this ground, we planted reeds and more greenbriers, and when they took hold, no one could see the building, and only the most inquisitive would venture into this thorny corridor.

While they were disassembling the buildings on the island for re-use of materials on the mainland, Willy and Bruce began the construction of two more boats. In the main room of the Inn, they built one for cargo, which would hold four people plus their goods, and a smaller, lighter one which might carry only two people and which could easily be dragged up on the marsh and hidden. Bruce was so intrigued by the latter that he immediately began the design of a third boat, incorporating certain changes which he felt would identify the boat as "his."

Chapter 19
Visiting Plans

Hope and I had agreed upon visits to each other's homes at specific times, at least four times a year, excepting for mid-winter when the bays might be frozen or full of drifting ice. This schedule was planned around a certain number of days after the full moon, just before the planting season, twice during the summer, and once after harvest.

We had agreed on a signal that would indicate to one another that it was safe to proceed. We each took a forked tree limb and impaled it horizontally in a steep bank where it could be easily seen along the route that each us would have to travel while visiting the other. His, near the mouth of the estuary on which he lived, and mine along the shoreline of our island at a place which he must pass on the way to our boat landing. Both limbs were weather beaten, and projected casually from the bank, as though the tide had left them there. Each branch had two limbs, one branch being much larger than the other. If there was danger, the limb impaled in the bank would be rotated so that the larger branch was moved to point at the sky. It was a signal known only to us. It seldom worked since the weight of ice would gather on the limb and rotate it to a different position.

Hope and Rosanne kept us supplied with a particular type of tasty nut which could not grow on the island because of the tree's dislike of salt air. Eleena was attempting to weave a cloth from the fibers of a certain grass which had an affinity for the sea side of the bluffs of Howling Head. The House of Thorns continued to prosper, being now divided into two sleeping areas, for they had another child, a son, whom they named "Mars" after a planet of the night sky.

Chapter 20

The House at the Spring

When Willy was several years older, he, too, expressed a desire to have his own house. He chose to restore a small farmhouse which had stood by the fresh water pond which, in turn, powered the waterwheel. The roof on the one-story building had collapsed and the window glass had fallen from the frames.

"I can put a thatched roof on the house, if you will help me raise the main beams. We can fill in most of the windows, and repair the ones on the east side, which catch the morning sun. There is a field of rich soil, but it is so overgrown that it will have to be burned off to kill all the trees which have taken root. We can use the trunks from some of them for roof rafters," Willy continued. "Living closer to the waterwheel will help me to find the time to use the wheel more, and I can make more things to make life better for all of us." I could find no flaw in his reasoning, and was glad that he was not planning to leave the island. And so we collected all that was required. That which we could not find, Willy made for himself, nails and spikes and crudes saw blades which were used to fashion trees into lumber.

We chinked the cracks between the building logs with clay, and when the clay was dry, we painted it with melted beeswax. On a late autumn day, when the grasses in the field were dry and golden, and a fog bank hid the smoke from any eyes on the mainland, we burned the field. We carefully ignited small patches, working against the wind so that the fire would not get out of control, and with the breeze blowing away from the mainland so that the smoke would be neither smelled nor seen.

Around the base of each of the larger trees in the field we built a cone of twigs, so that the fire there would be particularly hot and long-lasting, killing the tree where it stood. When this project was completed, we had a blackened rectangle of earth, full of stubble, but ready to be turned over, one spade full at a time, and planted. The stumps could be dug out later, or left to rot

Willy had little interest in farming, growing barely enough for his needs, preferring to spend his time shaping the hot metal. The objects that he fashioned he shared with the rest of us, and, in return, was supplied with all of the food from the sea or from the field that he needed. He made traps, snares, hooks, and fine knives, sharpened to an almost mirror finish, with wooden handles carefully wrapped in deerskin. It was a fine arrangement. We saw him often, and he enjoyed the independence of his craftsmanship.

Willy, he of the coarse black hair and gapped teeth, was our resident mechanical genius. He was a miracle worker with even the most primitive of equipment. Those pieces of machinery which he could not salvage from the ruins around us, he would invent for himself. His swarthy face contorted in concentration, his unkempt hair pointing in all directions, he would strive to solve a problem which intrigued him and might be useful to all of us.

With information gleaned from the omnivorous reading of the books to be found scattered among the buildings of the village he was able to build a smelter and a forge, with which he melted and shaped scrap pieces of lead, copper and other metals.

This hot liquid was made to flow into molds of dry clay, and when the metal had cooled and hardened, the clay was chipped away, leaving the metal shaped in the form of the cavity which had been made in the clay. In this manner objects were formed, from bowls to gears to large nails, the only limitations being the imagination of the craftsman and the type and amount of metal to be heated and the weight of the molds and finished castings.

If Willy could not form the piece by casting, he would shape the part by heating flat strips of metal in the flames of the forge, and then cut and hammer them into the required configuration.

In this way, the water wheel was refined, and the force of the falling water drove gears, which in turn drove saw blades, grindstones and drills, the use of which permitted easier construction of still more devices. The smelters were built along the beachfront, in vertical clefts in the face of the cliffs which formed natural chimneys, once the open side that faced the sea had been walled in with clay and rocks. The chimney was then filled from the top of the cliff with layers of hot-burning charcoal which he made himself, sea shells ground to a powder and pieces of the metal to be melted. A basin was placed in the bottom of the chimney and the fire was lit in the lower end. As the fire was drawn up into the shaft by natural draft, it became hotter and hotter, melting the raw pieces of metal included in the chimney, which then flowed back down through the embers and collected in the basin. From this basin, the metal flowed out by gravity through channels and into the clay mold.

This work was often brutal. The gathering of the metal, the cutting and transporting of the firewood for making charcoal, clay and rocks for chimneys and molds, and the handling of the fiery hot metal fell upon the shoulders of my middle son. The realization of his inventions by the sweat of his brow and calluses of his hands was his reward. He was only an average hunter and fisherman, and a mediocre farmer, but he was an outstanding creative individual whose work enriched our lives in ways that would be impossible to measure.

With the skill of a jeweler, Willy also fashioned delicately inlaid knives and fish spearing points, the latter pierced to accept a line which could be used to haul in a creature which was too large to be immediately landed by the use of the harpoon shaft, alone. The shafts themselves were carefully carved and polished, so that the simple act of holding such a tool in ones' hand was in itself a celebration of the art of the hunt.

His hands and forearms were as scarred by the splashing of the hot metal and nicked by the jagged scraps which he handled, as though he might personally have fought the beasts which his tools killed. There were only Bruce, Eleena and myself sharing our room-within-a-room now, and so we decided to close up the doorway to the sleeping quarters that had been used by Rosanne and the twins, giving us less space to care for. We could easily open it again when they visited us. Bruce enjoyed the luxury of a private room, but spent more and more time away, fishing or hunting, sometimes helping Willy as his apprentice and spending the night at the Spring House with him. They planned to construct an ice house on the bank above the pond, burrowing into the ground horizontally, and shoring up the roof with logs. When the pond froze, it would be much easier to cut the ice into manageable blocks and store them underground right there, than to carry them away immediately. Later, when the stream had thawed, the blocks could be extracted from the tunnel and floated downstream towards the Inn.

Eventually, Aquarius joined Willy at the farmhouse. At first being very reluctant to leave her family, she soon became accustomed to the roominess and privacy which she had not been able to enjoy in the cramped confines of the House of Thorns. Aquarius and Willy named their first child, also a girl, "Faith."

Bruce spent more time than ever in the woods and on the water, beginning to recognize his own needs and develop his special skills.

Chapter 21
The Nightmare

One morning, early in the spring, when the ice had begun to break up in the harbor, Willy appeared at our door at The Inn, out of breath from having run the long distance from the spring house. In an agitated voice, he said,

"I am afraid for Hope and Rosanne. Aquarius woke up this morning from a nightmare about her twin sister, Aries." Pausing for breath, he began again.

"Something has happened at the House of Thorns. She could not remember the dream, only her sister's voice, calling to her for help, and a feeling of great cold, as though she herself was on the ice. Aquarius has had a terrible premonition of disaster.

"We must go and find them as soon as possible. The drifting ice is so thick in the bay that we will have to wait until it clears. It may refreeze and lock us in until we can't row, swim or walk. We all want to go now but we must be patient. Maybe it is only a bad dream, I said, hoping that was true. I'll start to get the boat ready," Willy said, "and we can leave as soon as the water is ice-free."

He tipped the boat right-side-up from where it had been stored, and dragged it to the edge of the launching area. It gave him something to do, but the rest of us felt powerless. There was nothing to do but wait for the thaw.

"You and I will go, Willy. Do you think it would be better if Aquarius and Faith came down here to stay with Eleena and Bruce?" I suggested.

"That might be a good idea. They will be a comfort to each other. Bruce, that means you will be the man of the house until we return with some good news, we will bring some new treats and tell you that everything is all right. What do we have to take to them?" I asked. We prepared a list of items which they would welcome after the long winter. We speculated on how much the children had grown, and what new discoveries they must have made in their surroundings, which were still exotic, mysterious to us, and dangerous.

"He knew that it was dangerous when he decided to live there. Why did we let him go?" questioned my wife.

"It was his decision, agreed to by Rosanne. They knew the risks, and did their best to protect themselves."

"Look, maybe this worrying is all for nothing, and Aquarius's dream was only that, a bad dream," I said. "I hope so, I hope so," prayed Eleena. When most of the ice had cleared, Willy and I, side by side at the oars, departed from Howling Head. Our cargo included staple supplies and treasures which we knew they would enjoy, as well as a shotgun and some precious shells which we had hoarded for such an event. The shells were so old now that I had no idea if they would even fire. As it turned out, the gun was unnecessary. As we entered the mouth of the creek, I looked for the forked tree branch which would be a signal to us if there was trouble, but it was not there. Perhaps the ice had carried it away. There was no movement to greet us; no smell of wood smoke. The lodge was surrounded by rotting ice, which, shaded by the dense growth all around, melted more slowly than the ice in the open water. The trap door in the floor beneath the building stood open, and the building was empty. All of the contents had been removed, so that the interior was more barren than it was when we first discovered it. Thinking that there might be some clues to the disappearance of this part of my family, I searched under the ice around the pilings on which the building stood. We cut several holes and peered into the dark water, but saw nothing. Nor was there any sign of the boats, which had been hidden nearby in the brush.

. The soft ice, weakened by the holes which we had cut, groaned and sagged beneath our weight, so that we were forced to retreat to our boat. The one weakness of the House of Thorns was that no one had anticipated the problem of the ice. In the bitter cold of winter anyone could walk across the pond and stand directly beneath the building, to do whatever they wanted, including the threat of fire.

There was no sign of any force used against the trap door although it appeared to be lightly scorched. The threat of fire, like a hot torch held against the belly of the building, might have been enough to bring Hope and his family to the point of surrender. I wondered, "Was it that, or did they chose for some yet unknown reason, to move voluntarily, and plan to contact us later?" There were so many questions, and no answers. Willy and I spent several hours in the vicinity, even proceeding upstream for several miles. The area seemed unfamiliar now, but I thought that I saw the remains of an old camp fire on a knoll.

Since the tide was beginning to run out, we decided it was best to depart. We considered leaving a note for Hope and his family, but reasoned that it would serve no good purpose, only disclosing our existence to others. Hope and Rosanne knew where we were, and that we cared about them, and that they could find refuge with us. In great sadness, we returned to Howling Head.

Chapter 22
Bruce the Hunter

Bruce took his boat for one last duck hunting trip in the late winter. Reluctantly, as I had promised, and with deep concern for his safety, I had given him the shotgun and two precious shells so that he could test fire them and perhaps determine if the remainder of the shells, which we had carefully hoarded, would still fire. Any other game would have to be caught with the decoys and baited lines. Taking along a bucket of small minnows and cut clams he made his way to a raised section of the old roadbed on a slightly higher island of salt marsh halfway to the mainland. There was a pond on the lee side of the road, sheltered from the wind by the lush growth which now followed the road bed. The roadbed itself was several feet above the normal high tide, and thus collected seeds of all kinds which drifted into it, or were deposited by birds which found refuge there.

Arriving at the selected site on a rising tide, Bruce pulled the boat up on the bank and started to stalk any birds which were resting in the pond, which was a hundred yards away. His first thought was to try to shoot at a flock of birds swimming close together, killing as many as he could on the water with his precious first shotgun shell. He would chase any cripples down on foot, if possible without using the precious second shell. Then he would take his catch back to the boat, exchanging the dead birds for his decoys, which he would carry back and place in the pond. With the remaining shell he would attempt to kill a flying bird on the wing, a luxury that only a true hunter could afford, since the shells on Howling Head were almost gone. He had read enough about hunting to know how highly prized the art of wing shooting once was, and he was determined to have his chance, even if was with only one shot. He did as he had planned, surprising a flock of ducks swimming in the pond and killing five with the first shell. He carried them back to the boat and returned with the decoys

    He placed the decoys in the pond beside the roadway, baiting the hooks and then hiding the boat some distance away. Staying hidden in some brush near the decoys, he raised the gun in practice and trained it on many flying birds. Safety on, he put his finger on the trigger, the gunstock to his cheek and pivoting to follow the birds as they flew in from all angles, calculating the lead, he tried to remember all that he had read. Birds landed and fed among the decoys, and he could see them trying to escape the hooks. He put the gun down and went to the pond to dispatch the ducks which had become caught and to re-bait the hooks.

    The tide had come in, and he moved the stakes which anchored the decoys to higher land. He went back to his hidden position on the road. Off in the distance, moving toward him, just a few feet above the marsh, was a line of geese. He could hear their calls, faint against the wind at first, but growing more distinct as they struggled to reach the pond. Their clamor grew louder and more excited as they approached.

    He had never killed a goose. They always seemed to be much too wary to be attracted to his lures. But he longed to bring one down, somehow, and present the rich, feathery down that they wore to Rosanne, so that she could stuff some warm garment with it.

On they came, changing course to take advantage of the wind or every little shelter from it. He crouched lower, huddled against the shrubbery, hardly daring to blink lest they see his movement and flare, catching the wind in their wings and riding it quickly out of range. Closer they came, sliding off to his left, then veering back to the right, and suddenly they were straight ahead of him, wings cupped to land among the decoys. Their murmuring ended as they concentrated on settling into the pond in front of him. What a perfect opportunity! He clicked the safety off and drew a bead on a goose heading just to his left. As he rose to shoot, the flock wheeled at the sight of him, and as he pulled the trigger, with the muzzle of the gun pointed two feet ahead of the flight path of his intended victim, a second bird appeared from nowhere and was struck by the same shot.

"Two for one," Bruce shouted, as one bird dropped like a stone.

"They'll never believe it." The second goose behind the first wavered in flight, but did not fall immediately. Its erratic flight carried it into the thicket along the roadbed, where it disappeared into the brush. He ran after it, sending up splashes of spray from the tide, which had now risen almost to the remnants of the driftwood logs. Out of the corner of his eye he saw his boat floating away with the breeze. In the excitement of the hunt he had forgotten to secure it. He could not recover it in the deepening water and it continued to drift, moving quicker in the breeze.

The water rose higher, beginning to cover the grass in which he stood and rising over the stakes which held the decoys, so that he could not retrieve them without getting wet, which he did not want to do. The temperature was falling, the tide was still rising, and it was late afternoon.

He passed the spot where the crippled goose had fallen, and saw a broken wing fluttering in the brush. He reached in and grabbed a handful of feathers. With much noisy flapping, he pulled the goose away from its hiding place. It did not appear to be hard hit, but a smear of blood on its cheek indicated a hit there. He laid the bird on the ground at his feet, where it remained without moving, murmuring softly to itself. He moved his hands around its head, in front of its eyes, but there was no response to the movement. The goose was blind! A single non-lethal pellet had passes through its head and destroyed its sight.

Filled with unexpected compassion, he picked up the wounded bird, and, with great gentleness, cradled it in his arms. The bird did not struggle. Bruce looked for higher ground along the road, the goose's unseeing head falling quizzically over his shoulder as he walked, its feathers rumpled by the wind. It made no effort to escape. He reached the highest point of the roadbed. The water never quite reached it. Being higher, the land was more exposed to the wind and thus colder. The temperature continued to fall. His boat continued to drift away.

Sometime in that night or the next, for it took two days to find him, he had laid down next to a large log which had drifted there, to seek shelter from the freezing blasts of wind. He had cradled the goose under his jacket with his hands under its wings for the last bit of warmth, and both died of exposure. We brought them both back to the island, and buried them together in the tiny graveyard next to the ruins of the chapel. Willy had fashioned a crude copper cross, melting the remains of a copper roof into a clay mold, cast from the corroded remains of the emblem under which Elena's' former captors were buried.

Life is sadder without Bruce. We never knew when he would appear, or what delicacies he would bring us. We did know that sooner or later, he would appear, and that he would bring us something. Once in a while it was only a smile and an appetite, but those were exceptional days. Life is harder now, without him, which is a compliment to the passing of any man. He will not be back again. Eleena and I will miss him dearly.

Chapter 23
Alone Again, Disasters

Willy works listlessly at his forge...We have more than we need of things that we can make or gather for ourselves. What we need is cloth and thread; what we have is metal goods, waterfowl, green vegetables and all manner of seafood. It is regrettable that Hope and Rosanne were not able to establish friendly trade with those others who live on the mainland. We have a need for each other, a need which is buried beneath fear and greed and ignorance. We hope that they have somehow survived and that someday we will all meet again. Eleena works more slowly, spending time at Willy's and Aquarius's house, doting on the child, Faith. The two of them often went berry picking or beachcombing.

Faith was delighted with each curious object which the sea presented to her. They are a private pair, perfectly matched except in age, Eleena sees herself mirrored in her adopted granddaughter, and with Faith happily absorbing everything that she is being taught.

The smoldering ember had probably been there among the damp straw roof for some time before night fell. Willy had raked the overflowing ashes from the forge, dampened the hot ground with water from the stream, and sent a cloud of sparks and steam rising into the damp air. The family had eaten their evening meal, and then gone to bed when night fell. Willy had closed the sheet metal shutters over the front door to keep out the dampness, and then fell asleep himself. In the night, a breeze sprang up and fanned the single glowing ember which had drifted onto the thatched roof, until the dry thatch burst into a flame that quickly enveloped the house. It did not take long for the burning roof to fall in on them. I can only hope that they died of smoke inhalation before the fire reached them. There was no evidence that any of them tried to escape. It was a heartbreaking catastrophe.

We who survive are devastated. I sealed the building by closing the metal shutters that Willy had made. Eleena and I did not go to the Spring House again. Willy's forge grew cold. No longer did the sound of his hammer ring out across our settlement. After a while the vines grew over everything, finding the rough stones to their liking, until they almost disappeared from sight, but not from our thoughts.

The bright sparks and hot metal which Willy found so attractive were his undoing. I comfort myself by thinking it is possible that somewhere in Heaven he is forming halos of gold, while Faith and Aquarius keep patient watch by his side, as they have always done. With the dying of the forges' embers, the world of Howling Head has grown colder. Eleena and I huddle closer together, more than ever before seeking the lost warmth of our children and their families. There were now only the two of us.

Several months later while helping me to pull the boat from the water after searching for shellfish in the bay, Eleena stepped on a sharp fish bone which was hidden in the mud. The jagged sliver, which was covered with rotted flesh, pierced her moccasin, and was driven deeply into the sole of her foot. I could not control the resulting infection. I remembered the care which I had given her when she was recovering from her gunshot wounds, and tried to repeat that success, but the bacteria laden bone had stabbed too deeply for me to drain the wound. Her leg became grossly swollen and there was nothing that I could do to ease her agony. After a long, painful illness, during which she cried out for our dead children, she awoke, pale and lucid, without pain, but dying. "I am so sorry to be leaving you," she whispered. "Go in peace and find our children. Tell them that I love them and wish to be with them. I will meet them again on the other side. I promised to tell them.

"Will you be all right?" she asked of me.

"No, I can't stay here without you. What is the purpose of being here, if all of you are gone? Why must it be this way, my wife? Why? We have tried so hard to make our lives successful here, in spite of the hardships"

I cried, but she made no reply. When I looked down at her face again her eyes were closed and her breath had ceased. She was at peace. I buried her in the grave in the churchyard with the others, wrapped in the best of the women's clothes that I could find. There were two rough crosses remaining of the group that Willy had cast, and so I marked his mother's grave with one, and drove the other into the ground in the plot next to hers...It would be mine.

I must to leave this desolate island.

I think that I am going insane.

I am alone!

I had forgotten Dr. Brislow's magic medicine, I am going insane.

Chapter 24
The Wreck in the Dunes: *The Scorpion*

In the spring of the year, I explored once more the empty cellar of the Long Boat Inn. Stored away and buried in a remote corner I found several black bottles of strange liquor. The labels had long since disintegrated so I had little idea of the contents. From the open bottle came a tantalizing fragrance. Carefully taking a drink, I was astonished by the captivating taste. Taking the bottle with me I grew warmer as I stood, undecided about my next direction. I decided to walk the beach, having suddenly become more alert and anxious to see what new treasures the waves might have left for me.

    I walked along the surf line as the light began to fail. I heard a twittering sound from a place higher on the beach. Investigating, I found a flock of sandpipers gathering together to spend the night huddled in a coil of hemp anchor line. As the drowsy birds settled for the evening I saw that the loose end of the line extended up and away and disappeared into the dunes. I followed the line for as long as I could in the fading light, stopping my search only when it disappeared beneath the side of a large dune. I vowed to return the next day with a shovel and continue to seek the other end of the mysterious anchor line. Each day the wind and water altered the appearance of the shoreline, so I was not sure what to expect in the early morning. What I did find, exposed by the wind, was a dark mass, a ship's hull hidden behind still other dunes, covered for many years by bayberry, dune grasses and goldenrod. Over the next few days the forces which had hidden the wreck there, the wind and drifting sand, reversed and exposed more of it to me.

The beach stretched from the edge of the waves to the beginning of the dunes, which grew higher as they retreated to the center of the beach on which they existed. Covered with vegetation, the size of the dunes ebbed and flowed with the intensity of the wind and waves, which either built them higher or tore them down. As I walked along I looked up from the water's edge to the dunes and began to see the stark, dark structure among the hills of sand. I took another drink from the black bottle and made my way up and into the sandy terrain.

Partially uncovered by the wind was the hull of an old wooden ship. Looking forward and aft from the point where I stood, I could make out the shape of the complete vessel, resting upright but partially camouflaged by brush and hidden by sand. As I walked around the hull, I saw that the ships' name, faintly painted on the stern and bow were the weathered words "The Scorpion."

Climbing onto the deck and peering into an open hatch cover I saw that dim light was entering the hull through round glass skylights fitted into the overhead deck planking, as well as through several portholes along the sides of the hull. I discovered that the ship's hold was divided into three sections, each of which could be entered by means of deck hatches which were partially buried under wind-blown sand which had drifted onto the deck. A small sleeping compartment all the way in the bow was hidden from my view. The three cargo holds could also be inspected and loaded through doors in the bulkheads which separated them.

In the first hold were a piano and other musical instruments. I took another sip from my bottle and, placing it on the piano, struck a simple note on the keyboard. The note reverberated throughout the ancient planks. The loose sand fell down from the skylights and shrunken deck planks. The sky outside grew lighter and the roar of the ocean diminished to a gentle sigh.

Having never played the piano, I accidently struck a chord, a magnificent sound which began to shake sand away from the outer hull of the vessel. I played on, though I had never been taught as a musician, with the sea gloriously calm, with white gulls wheeling silently overhead, seemingly entranced by the miraculous melodies which now flew from my fingers in the interior of the stricken ship.

By sunset I had finished the dark bottle. The last notes that I struck brought forth a glorious sunset which lingered long enough for me to make my way unsteadily home along the water's edge.

At last home in my own bed, I fell into a deep, timeless sleep. When I awakened in the morning and had eaten, for I was very hungry, I thought again of the mysterious wreck in the dunes. Taking another bottle from the hiding place in the cellar and opening it, I drank again. I hastily made my way to the shoreline, for I was not certain whether my memory was functioning correctly or whether I was hallucinating, I saw again the outline of the old hull in the dunes.

Entering the hatch and descending into the first hold, I saw now that the piano keys were warped and stained, and that sand had sifted through the dried out deck planking above and begun to fill the hold.

Entering into the second hold, I saw, placed on an artist's easel, a blank canvas, some brushes, and several paint tubes of various colors. I sipped from the bottle. Though I had never painted before, I took a brush full of clear blue pigment and painted a beautiful sky on the canvas, though I was not an artist. The overcast morning sky outside became cloudless and the sea ran smooth and flat along the beach. Warm sunlight spread across the shoreline and bathed the beach in a glorious glow. I touched a brush full of pink and tan pigments to the canvas, depicting where the sand and water's edge would be. As I looked through a porthole to the sea a mermaid appeared from the waves and made her way across the sand towards me. She entered the hull and made her way to where I stood.

She stood wordlessly before me, admiring my painting. She was breathtakingly beautiful and I was so lonely. We made love and instantly, as I painted, she bore our beautiful child. I took another, deeper taste of my drink. The brush fell from my hand, leaving an ugly smear of paint on the deck. The vision ended. Our child and her mother fled from me, across the beach toward the sea. Taking another brush full of carelessly colored muddy paint, I touched it to the area of my canvas which depicted the sea. The sea outside became violently agitated. My lovely mermaid, depicted on my canvas, withered like seaweed, washed up and dried in the hot sun. Her scaly tail became thin seashells which shattered as they fell from my canvas onto the hard deck beneath my feet. Then there was no trace of her or our child. I took a deeper drink.

In panic I painted furiously, the paint becoming thicker and the colors even more murky. The sky outside darkened. The waves grew and broke furiously upon the beach. Stinging sand, driven by a sudden wind, began to enter the wreck through the shrunken planks. In desperation I tried to wipe the paint from the canvas, until the canvas became a smear of dark grays, which matched the deepening twilight. I left the wreck, walking in a steady rain and returned to my room in the Long Boat Inn.

Again, after having slept exhaustedly for a length of time, I awoke, fuzzy headed and confused. I made my way once more to the wreck.

Now the old hull looked more desolate than ever. I entered the third compartment which was now more illuminated than ever, the wind having swept the sand away from the overhead glass and exposed more of the portholes. This hold contained a large open storage chest and a series of smaller containers. Each was filed with gold coins, pearls and jewels of all description. I spent the day drinking and examining the fortune which was before me. As evening fell I filled my pockets and every opening in my clothing with gold coins and jewels. I was overcome with greed. I decided to take as much of these riches with me as possible. I filled my ragged pockets until they would hold no more. I found an empty metal chest and filled it to the brim but it was too heavy to carry. I took a smaller chest which I could carry and decided to return in the morning for even more riches. The smaller chest was so full of treasure that I had trouble snapping it shut, having to sit on it before I heard the lock click, at which point I realized that I had no key to open it. Taking one last sip and staggering under the weight of the box and with my pockets overflowing, I made my way along the beach, gold and jewels falling from my clothing. In the morning I would return along this shining path, back to the wreck, using the pieces of sparkling lost treasure glowing in the rising sun as a trail marker. During this visit I would explore the small forward compartment in the bow of the hull.

Sweet sleep caressed my aching soul and body until hunger drove me out of bed. I went first to the basement of the Inn, searching, all uninvestigated corners for more of the mysterious, wonderful, beverage. But only two bottles remained and

I hoarded them. I searched the ragged clothes which I had worn to the wreck, and which were strewn about my room, hoping to examine my new wealth more closely in the daylight. There were only pebbles and bit of seashells. My pockets were full of holes, and perhaps the treasure had fallen out as I made my way home. Surely I could retrace my steps and recover much of the riches along the surf line. I hid the locked metal treasure box in a secret place.

It was several days before I felt well enough to return to the beach. I made my way again to the wreck, sober and aching with both excitement and sorrow. I had expected to return along a trail of spilled riches sparkling in the sun along the beach, but it was only pebbles and shells that I found. The wreck was also gone. The wind and sea had reclaimed the high dunes. There was only a long sand bar where once the high dunes had held the old hull captive. What the sea had captured and given to me, the sea had stolen away. I was alone again in an empty world. It was time to leave this desolate place. Where had the treasure gone? Damn the black bottles!

Chapter 25
The Whirlpool (Leaving)

It was an early foggy morning and uncertain preparations were made. I took my rowboat that was stored in a dilapidated shed above the tide line, and pulled it to the waters' edge. I furnished it with clothing in which I wrapped several glass jars, tightly sealed, and filled with valuable seeds, from which could be grown beautiful flowers or rare and hardy vegetables. I also included several magnifying glasses which could be used as fire starters, and wrapped the leather case which held the special vials that I had found in Dr. Brislow's cellar in a belt around my waist.

I carried the metal chest, shaking it from time to time, hearing the sound of the mysterious contents within, hoping that it would make a suitable peace offering to anyone that I encountered. I had no shells left for the gun, and no desire to fight and so I left it behind. I would join in peace whoever I met as a friend or they would kill me.

I stood in the sand, ready to launch, looking out of the harbor to the sea, which was as smooth as glass. I was tempted to ignore my concern of the open sea and instead of going inland, to row toward the horizon and let the sea decide my fate. Then I thought again of the warmth and comfort that might be possible among the people who dwelt on the mainland. Perhaps I would find my son, Hope, and his family. I decided to wait one more day, letting my choice of direction depend on the winds of chance, whether I was traveling to the mainland or to the sea. My Grandfather's rocky sun dial indicated that spring had arrived and the full spring tides were flowing. They could, if timed right, carry me far inland with minimum of rowing effort.

The following morning, Midnight the crow and I launched the boat into the inlet at first light. Fog had crept in from the sea, wiping out the sighting of all landmarks and leaving me with no idea of my progress, whether I was traveling toward the highlands or toward the sea. Midnight perched quietly on the bow, as blind as I was, turning his head first to the right and then to the left, and then staring back at me as though asking me if I could see something that he could not see. "Did I know where we were going?" he seemed to be asking. I sensed a slow, deliberate, circular movement of the water in which we floated.

There had been a tremor of the rock below the island, cracking some of the town's walls, breaking some panes of window glass in the remaining buildings and sending plumes of dust falling down from the corners of the cobwebbed ceilings. Somewhere beneath us a huge cavity had been opened in the bedrock of the earth below, not very noticeable on the surface, but Midnight and I would soon participate in an amazing result on the surface.

Trapped in the fog, traveling in the current, the boat was carried slowly at first in a wide circle which I could not see but could only feel. Faster and faster, we were carried by the growing, speedy movement of the water. Closer and closer we were drawn to the swirling center of a whirlpool. I could not row fast enough to escape. As our boat was pulled nearer to the dark, mysterious hole in the harbors' water which led into the depths of the maelstrom, I clung to the boats' wooden frame. Midnight found a secure perch on the bow, clinging to the anchor line cleat.

As we were drawn deeper beneath the surface and into the depths, the swirling tunnel of air through water in which we were captured became narrower and faster. In the dark depths surrounding us, illuminated at first only by the light from the foggy sky above the surface that passed through the deepening water around us swam thousands of flashing jellyfish and other small creatures.

Large and small, each glowing with pulsating lights of many colors, they flickered in unison with each faint vibration of the water slapping against our hull. Fish and other marine creatures, both huge and minute, were also drawn around our ever narrowing hollow tunnel. They watched us as well as the large sharks that pursued them, charging into view as though to pierce the walls of our air filled column, accidently or on purpose, then almost gaining access to us, but turning away at the last moment with a toothy mouthful of smaller, bloody prey.

As I peered in horror into the depths ahead of us, I saw the terrifying sight of a giant octopus, whose tentacles were wrapped around the narrowing exterior walls of the whirlpool, and whose hungry, beaked mouth was open to receive our boat and its contents. I drew back in terror, leaning against the wooden planks of the boat as though to become one of them, but there was no place to go. The octopus could not crush the walls of our shelter and it disappeared into the deeper water.

Suddenly, as quickly as it had sucked us under, the whirlpool slowed, the diameter of the tube which enclosed us increased and we were expelled to the surface, which was still shrouded in fog.

From somewhere close by came the soft cry of a woman weeping. It was difficult to locate the source as in the stillness of the mist it seemed to come from all directions. I rowed slowly, listening carefully. The fog muffled the sound and frustrated my efforts to find her. The fog thinned slightly and the sound of the damaged distant bell buoy reached us through the mist. At last, a glimpse of the distressed woman appeared. She was seated alone in a tiny boat, dressed in white gown, barely visible in the pale mist.

Sighting my own boat she stood up and in silence pointed in a direction which she obviously wished me to go. Taking to the oars again I did my best to comply with her instructions, rowing toward her, but when I turned to look for her again, she had vanished into the fog. I paused and listened for the sound of her weeping. There was only the faint, far away, sound of the bell buoy.

Night fell. Although the mist was lifting, I was still lost, now having drifted far out into the open sea, carried by the falling tide. The tolling of the bell buoy had faded away. I fell again into a deep, dreamless sleep. A sudden movement beneath the boat rocked it and awakened me. Small, shiny fish, gleaming in the faint star light from the sky and terrorized by something below them began to shower into the boat. Midnight quickly ate his fill, for we had not eaten in some time.

The boat was shaken again by something larger alive beneath it striking the hull. Another shower of silvery creatures flew from the sea and onto the deck. Dark fins broke the surface of the water around the boat and I was sharply aware that it was sharks pursuing the smaller fish which flew aboard in panic. I stabbed at the sharks with an oar each time that they came near enough, until, well fed, they disappeared into deeper water. We continued our long, directionless drift in the dark.

From our position on the sea I could hear the sound of waves breaking along a shoreline. A quickly moving thunderhead passed over our heads and moved across the shore, momentarily blanking out the stars and drenching us. There was a flash of lightning over the nearby land mass and for a second I glimpsed a gleaming white building, built on a hill which overlooked the sea where we were passing. The thunderhead passed by, and left the sky filled with brilliant white stars.

Chapter 26
Whale Island

Sometime during the night my companion, Midnight, and I drifted onto a wide, sandy beach. I pulled the boat high onto the sand, turned it on its side and propped it up with an oar. We slept on the sand beneath it. During the night, a gust of wind shook the hull, knocking down the prop, and for a few minutes we were trapped beneath it. I remembered Dr. Brislow. I thanked him! I took a sip from the blue vial stored on my belt and lifted the boat away from us.

Suddenly I thought of the good Dr. Brislow of Howling Head Island. He had treated my grandparents and me many times and had taken a liking to me, always curious about my sudden arrival as an infant on the island and suspecting something unusual. I would do odd jobs for him and run errands, so we were quite comfortable with one another. One day he took me aside and said "any that you feel alone or bewildered by your life, feel free to visit my home, whether I am here or away. You may read my medical books and any records that I have of treatment that I have advised for you or your grandparents. You may read my medical books and share in any treatments that I have advised for you or your grandparents. If all else fails and you are still troubled, go to my wine cellar and browse. There are secret cures for hidden maladies, some of which have no physical symptoms. I hope that this knowledge will be of use to you someday, even if I am gone. I had made my way down the narrow stairs, looking cautiously around the cellar. It was illuminated by only a single cobweb covered window, At first I could see only the empty wine bottles, returned to their racks...Then there were small wooden chests of drawers, each drawer holding an array of small medical instruments, though some held only scraps of paper with illegible handwriting. Nothing of importance was apparent to me.

The floor of the cellar was paved with pieces of flagstone of many sizes, each carefully selected for smooth appearance and fitted to its neighbor. As I explored I felt one of the stones moving beneath my feet. Getting down on my hands and knees I was able to lift the stone for its setting. In the cavity below I found a tarnished silver tray. Triangular in shape, in three separate compartments were three glass vials, each containing a liquid of a different color.

Instructions in Dr. Brislow's handwriting were in a faded envelope. "There is a cushioned leather belt with three pockets to hold these vials and protect them from damage. Wear the belt wherever you go and use the contents wisely for the following situations:

Red is for bravery: Take a sip when you feel that all is lost and you can' go on.

Gold is for healing and restoration: Take a sip for illness or use it as an ointment.

Blue is for strength: Use it when your own strength is not strong enough." And I had found a use for it! I took a sip and lifted the boat above us.

As we made their way from beneath the boat we were greeted by some of the inhabitants of Whale Island who were curious about our arrival on the beach. I explained our arrival as best I could. In return, they told us that the island on which we had landed was named "Whale Island" by its inhabitants, a gentle people who made their living by farming and fishing. The island rose higher to its hilly center and had well-kept fertile fields and forests. A sheltered harbor provided safe access to and from the sea. Seams of clay provided material for their fine pottery crafts. The climate was moderated by warm sea temperatures and gentle winds. They were at peace with the world. The island was somewhat remote and they had little contact with the rest of the world, which accounted for their curiosity about us.

The name "Whale Island" was rightfully given to the land. The islanders, known for their successful fishing industry, had, at one time, successfully hunted and killed whales for their meat, which was eaten. Nothing from the whales was wasted. Their thick blubber was boiled down into oil, which was used as fuel for their lamps, the teeth were carved into decorative objects, the bone and baleen, used for building and any scraps which remained were used for fertilizer on the prosperous farms fields.

A truce was reached with the whales. If any whales became sick or injured they were encouraged to enter the harbor, where they would be protected from predators and fed by the Islanders until they either were healed, in which case they were allowed to swim away, or died, in which case they were used for the Islanders' traditional purposes. In exchange, if any whale saw a human in distress on the sea, the whale would do it's best to bring the human to the safety of the harbor on Whale Island.

When we were rested, we were taken to the magnificent white building which we had glimpsed from the sea, to meet the ruler of the land.

Chapter 27
Hannah the Queen is Found

John and Midnight were taken to the castle to meet the Queen, who sat on a bleached white whalebone throne in her castle, which was positioned to look out over the sea. She was magnificent, as she sat upon her throne, surrounded by her subjects. Her long, graying hair was draped over her shoulder, partially hiding her face. She leaned toward John, and he saw something familiar about her, though he was uncertain what it was. Then he recognized her as the woman in white who had directed him when he emerged from the whirlpool.

She spoke. "You do not know me, John Kettle, but I know you from long ago." With that, she drew back her hair from her face and exposed a long, disfiguring scar which ran from her neck and across her cheek. Upon seeing the scar, both John and her subjects drew away from her, so terrible was the old wound. He knew then that she was his childhood love, Hannah, of Howling Head Island. He replied softly, "It has been so long. I have thought about you and that terrible accident every day of my life. So much has happened to both of us. I have brought you some gifts, although I didn't know if I would ever see you again. How did you get here?"

"My parents did not arrive at the tree clearing site where you were working, as you thought that they would. The noise that you heard was made by a group of excited tourists who did not even slow down to see what you had been doing.

Having no interest at the site where you had been clearing the stream, they continued toward the hill top, to picnic and to look out over the sea. I was on the ground in our bower where you left me, semiconscious and in great pain. I was unable to call out to them. I awoke some time later to the feeling of cold seawater flowing around me. The mournful sound of the howling dog, born on the wind, filled my ears as the gale increased.

A great wave covered the island. I was swept away from the bower which once we shared, and, as the wave receded, it carried me down into the bed of the stream. The stream, in turn, was filled with debris flowing down toward the harbor. I clung for my life onto a floating door that was entangled with other wreckage that had been wrested by the flood from the boat sheds and storage buildings above, torn open by the huge wave. Eventually the mass of wreckage on which I floated reached the harbor and continued to travel out into the open sea.

As I drifted, I could hear the sound of the bell buoy, which was the only clue to my whereabouts. The wreckage to which I clung trailed several long lengths of mooring lines that had been washed from their destroyed storage locations and which now trailed below the raft. Darkness fell, and I drifted again into a world of a painful sleep. There were no stars above, nor breeze on the surface of the now calm sea. The murmur of the bell grew fainter and disappeared, eventually drowned out by the sound of ripples lapping against my raft.

I awoke at the first faint light, stiff with cold and the pain from my bloody wound. A low mist hovered over the sea, which prevented me from seeing the distance in any direction. I could see that the raft was moving; there was a slight wake at that section of the door-raft which had now become the bow. At first I couldn't see how I was being propelled. As the day grew brighter and the water clearer, I saw that one of the lines that had been dangling beneath me was now extended straight out in front of my raft and was the cause of my movement. As the day grew lighter and the sunlight reached deeper into the clear sea water, I saw that I was being towed by a whale, whose tail was tangled in a mooring line that had once trailed below me.

We moved slowly. Looking at the back of the submerged leviathan, I could see that he was very old, shrunken from lack of food and injured. His skin was covered with white barnacles which stood out against his dark coloring, forming a unique pattern. A school of small sharks, sensing easy prey, attacked his bloody fins and lips. He was unable or unwilling to fight them off, or to even attempt to escape. His breathing was shallow. He barely surfaced .Never the less, we continued our journey.

The sun warmed our travels during the daylight hours. Among the debris which surrounded me on the raft was a supply of food and water in a picnic case, perhaps left by the passing tourists, for which I was very thankful. We continued on our mysterious voyage. Taking a long oar from among the wreckage on which I floated, I strove, with some success, to drive the sharks away from the nibbled flesh of my benefactor. After a period of travel across the uncharted sea, one evening, in the small hours of morning, we arrived at the whale's destination. We entered a shallow harbor in a strange land. We rested.

From the low hills which surrounded the harbor came curious people to greet the whale and myself. They poured containers full of small fish into the open mouth of the injured whale and after driving the few remaining sharks away, closed the entrance of the harbor with a floating barricade. We were safe.

The leaders of the people of "Whale Island" came down to help me onto the land. At first they were terrified of me and my appearance, keeping their distance even as they spoke to me. Though I had been washed by rain and seawater, my throat and face bore the terrible wound. My clothing was stained with my blood. The cloth was torn and ragged, filled with leaves and seaweed. My hair was wildly unkempt. I was glad that I didn't have a mirror or I might have regretted making it safely to land. I told them that I was injured in a storm.

The inhabitants of Whale Island are a gentle people whose existence has always depended on the sea. Over many, many years they have developed a special relationship with the great whales of the ocean, which once were their prey. Now, all and any whales in need were offered a safe harbor. Those whales that could be saved were protected and returned to good health. Those that were beyond help were allowed to die, and their remains salvaged to support the people of Whale Island. All blubber was removed and rendered into whale oil,, as it was many years ago, used for lamps and lubrication, any teeth were carved into jewelry and any bones were used in building a castle for the most honored citizen of the island, which to my, surprise became me.

The old whale has remained here, recovering, but never able to regain enough strength to survive in the open sea. It is kept well fed and safe by the islanders."

As they spoke, John remembered the words of Dr. Brislow, and the leather belt that he wore around his waist and which held the magic vials. On his fingertips he took a drop of the precious fluid from the golden vial and gently massaged Hannah's scarred face. The scar grew fainter and then, as everyone watched, completely disappeared. Her gray-streaked hair became jet black again. She was once again his childhood sweetheart. Without thinking, he touched his fingers to his own face, and the hard, weathered lines of his troubled life were also erased. He, too, was young again. He touched the wing of Midnight, and the crow could fly...

The watching crowd cheered and sang in approval of such a miracle. One single drop of the golden liquid remained in the vial, and John let it fall into the harbor where the old whale was resting. Immediately the whale's tattered fins were restored and his wrinkled skin became plump and healthy. He spouted a plume high into the air for all to see. The crowd was ecstatic!

The tumultuous crowd drew closer around them, anxious to see more of John and their Queen Hannah, and the gifts which he had brought to their island.

John opened the containers of new seeds which he had saved, describing the useful plants which could be grown from them. They were anxious to plant them, and see the potential benefits as food, medicine or beauty. He distributed the magnifying glasses and they were very happy to have their search for fire to be made so much easier.

All that remained was the curious metal box. The crown grew closer around them as he tried to open it, but it was no use. Several of the strongest men in the group also tried to pry the lid open but it remained tightly closed. The crowd grew restless and John became more doubtful of the wisdom of bringing the box with him. Hannah sat, patiently waiting.

Thinking more clearly, John remembered the words of Dr. Brislow, and the vial which would supply strength when needed. Taking the blue vial from the pouch, he applied a drop to the lock of the unopened box and it immediately sprang open. All present gathered in curious awe as the contents were spread over the table between John and Hannah.

Only dusty shells and pebbles were strewn across the table. Not one gem or golden coin was showing. There was silence as the once noisy crowd grew silent and began to turn away. Midnight watched intently as he circled above them. John Kettle quietly cursed himself for the drunken stupor which had convinced him that he was bringing treasure as a gift. He began an apology to Hannah, but she sat, quietly watching him, and then said "Your presence in my life is all that I need. What good would a box of gold and jewels be to me? Now that you are here I have more than I could ever want. Thank you, my love."

And John replied, "My gracious, beautiful Hannah! Having lost you twice, I will never leave you again." Reaching into his pocket, he took out the tarnished brass bell which he had found in the needles beneath the evergreen tree. "Does this look familiar," he asked. She began to cry. Attached was a small faded fragment of the red bandana from which it once was suspended from a twig on the top of the tree. "It is even more marvelous than any gold coins or shiny gems. I am glad that you remembered and that you could find it again." Hannah replied.

As they sat together, looking over the collection of gifts from the sea, spread across the table, there was a movement from the inside of a large spiral shell which rested there having been spilled from the metal box. The shell was of rare "Mammoth Periwinkle." From the shell, a unique creature slowly emerged, shiny and wet. Growing larger as it moved from its cramped life in the shell, it crawled to the edge of the table, and slowly dried and unfurled its wings. Hannah held out her hand and the butterfly, growing larger, climbed on to it, flexing its wings as they dried. The wings were covered with a bright gold powder upon which appeared a dark purple star.

The creature was named a Purple Star Butterfly, after its appearance. It was so seldom seen that almost nothing was known of it, other than it was a forecaster of tremendous good fortune. It is believed that every seven years it emerges from a single egg which has been deposited in the empty shell of a Mammoth Periwinkle, itself a rare creature that has been washed up on the beach at high tide. Many of the needed empty shells are never found by the butterflies, while others that do contain an egg are washed back into the sea and the single egg is eaten by sea creatures before it can develop into a butterfly. Some shells containing an egg are taken high into the sky by seagulls, dropped onto a hard surface where the Periwinkle shell is shattered and the butterfly egg is eaten by the bird which found it. Hence the species was extremely rare. The crowd began to gather again.

The wings of a Purple Starred butterfly are coated with a dust of gold, as fine as pollen, which has been extracted from the seawater by the butterfly's larvae as it matures in the periwinkle shell. Hannah held out her hand, palm down, and the butterfly walked onto her smooth skin. She held out her hand to John, who in the same way held his hand next to hers. The butterfly climbed partially across the two hands and stopped, poised on both hands. It increased its wing beats to a blur, signifying that John and Hannah were joined together, two people into one, the King and Queen of Whale Island. The crowd roared with approval.

When the crowd had quieted down, the butterfly launched itself into the air above them, pausing above their heads to shower the new King and Queen of Whale Island with a dusting of gold. The recovered whale in the harbor spouted a giant plume which contained a small portion of the magic serum. The plume drifted over the crowd and fell upon them, healing everyone that it touched, bringing astonishment and joy to all.

The contents of the metal box, sand, seashells and pebbles were strewn carelessly on the ground, whereupon, the sharp eyed Midnight flew down from the great height where he had been watching. With his sharp eyes he found a large diamond that had been obscured by the debris in the box and presented it to Hannah as his wedding gift for the occasion.

Offshore, a pod of one hundred whales gathered, watching the ceremony with great interest and listening to the cheering crowd. When the searching Purple Starred Butterfly was ready to lay her egg she reached the beach and found the empty Mammoth Periwinkle shell that she needed. All of the whales spouted simultaneously. A brilliant rainbow, spreading from horizon to horizon, and reaching high into the sky, arched across the sea, bringing good fortune and happiness to all of the inhabitants of Whale Island.

The coronation, or perhaps the hallucination, was a completed.

The celebration continued long into the evening. Queen Hannah was momentarily distracted by an official of her court and John Kettle, after so many days of loneliness was overwhelmed by the crowds of excited party goers who surrounded him, and numbed by the wine which everyone was sharing. He wandered down to the darkened beach with Midnight on his shoulder. The sound of the revelers faded as they moved away. John and Midnight sat upon their boat, overwhelmed by the noisy revelry after years of silence.

Taking a moment to reflect upon the events on Whale Island, after some thought, John reached under the seat and withdrew the last of the dark bottles. They sat together in silent harmony, Midnight eventually tucking his head beneath his wing and sleeping, perched on the bow cleat, awaiting further action.

Finally, John pulled the boat to the edge of the sea, and after another swig from the bottle, launched it into the swift current that flowed beneath the surface of the calm water. They journeyed together again, riding the waves, watching as the glow in the sky from the events on Whale Island slowly disappeared behind them. Overhead, a multitude of brilliant stars observed their wandering. As they moved the stars became mere pin pricks in the black dome above their heads, and then, even those faint droplets of starlight disappeared all became quiet as they moved north at the mercy of the sea.

Chapter 28
The Return to Howling Head

The rowboat drifted aimlessly with its fatigued crew resting in the slow moving waters along the shoreline of Howling Head Island, near the empty wharfs of the Long Boat Inn. It momentarily touched the bank and then jolted along among the twisted pilings of the docks. some of which were in the process of being extracted from the mud by the ice of the long winter Exhausted, John Kettle was asleep in the bottom of the craft, with a few inches of water soaking through his clothing. An almost empty bottle of the intoxicating beverage which he had found in the Inn rolled around by his side. Midnight, the coal black crow, stood forlorn and hungry on the bow. A flock of wild crows watched their arrival with interest. They circled overhead, cawing to themselves at the strange sight of a crow being so close and unafraid of a human.

Stirring at last, John awakened, jarred by the chill and the erratic direction of his boat as it bounced among the logs. He sat up, shaking with cold. Hoping to warm himself, he again took a deep drink from the bottle, draining it. He managed to paddle the boat to a place where they could go ashore after tying the boat to a piling. Having done so, with Midnight on his shoulder, he made his way along the fading path to the old door of the Inn which he had opened and closed so many times before. There was no change in the main room, other than that a window glass high above had been broken, which let the cold weather in more easily. His small room remained intact and undisturbed. His open journal on the table was just as he had left it.

Shivering violently, he changed into dry clothing, emptying the meager contents of his pockets onto the table, throwing the wet clothing which he had been wearing to dry and leaving it on the floor outside. Now he needed to find some warmth. He found some dry kindling and attempted to start a fire in the old iron stove. There was one box of matches, saved for such an emergency, in a dry jar. His hands were shaking so violently that he could not pick a single match from the box. Several spilled upon the floor which had been dampened by his wet clothing. He held two matches together in his numbed hand and struck them on the box. They sputtered, and lit, but his nose was running so badly that drops of mucus fell on the flame and extinguished them, and also on the striker, which ruined it, at least until it was dry again. He was too cold now to continue. . Perhaps later in the day the sun would shine and he could use the remaining magnifying glass to generate a spark from which to light the stove. Choosing the warmest bedding and clothing which hung on the wall, he burrowed, naked and shivering violently, into the mound of dry cloth and tried to sleep.

But the sun did not shine for the remainder of that day, or the next. John Kettle remained almost motionless beneath the mound of clothing and bedding which covered him. Outside, the noisy flock of crows surrounded the building, having discovered a Great Horned Owl hiding in the woods. Flushed into the open and pursued by the multitude of angry black birds, the owl sought safety in the rafters of the Inn, gaining entrance through the broken window. The flock of crows circled low in a frenzy around the building, their calls attracting similar birds from as far away as the sound of their voices could be heard. Lower and lower they flew, circling the Inn. Louder and louder became their voices, more and more numerous their numbers. They gathered in a dense cloud around the overgrown Inn. They pecked at the remaining windows, but did not break them. Nor did they try to enter. Owls feast on crows, hunting them in the crow's roosts at night and so they feared for their own safety in the dim recesses of the Inn. In the faint light in the rafters of the Long Boat Inn the Great Horned Owl would have been the master of the darkness.

On the morning of the third day the crows circled the Long Boat Inn again, at first quietly and then showing their rising frustration with an increasing clamors. The owl appeared at the broken window through which it had entered, hoping that its enemies were not watching. Its appearance sent the crows again into a rage. They made one final attempt to flush it out, landing on the overgrown roof and pecking at the window frames. The attempt was successful. The Owl, flushed from the rafters, dropped silently from the broken window and on its hushed wings, coasted low to the ground. Hugging the browned grass it flew low into some dense evergreens. From there it escaped, always keeping thick foliage between it and its foes. The dark flock of crows surrounding the Inn circled noisily until sundown, and then vanished into a roost in the distant trees.

Dawn arrived. At last, under the layers of warm bedding John Kettle stirred. Outside, all was calm. The warm sun rose over a cloudless horizon and heated the sand at the water's edge. A creature climbed from a Mammoth Periwinkle shell that had washed up on the beach. It paused to unfold its wings and dry them in the glowing dawn before displaying their brilliant purple color. When it was ready, it flew from the sandy shore to the Long Boat Inn and circled above the door. It fluttered, again and again, and showered that entrance with golden dust.

Life began again on Howling Head Island.

Hidden by the glare of the rising sun on the sea, a sail appeared on the horizon. If the nameplate on the transom and bow of the distant boat could be read from afar it would be read as *The Scorpion's Widow.*

Chapter 29
The Story of *The Scorpions*

John could not believe his eyes when he looked over the sea from the heights of Howling Head Island. Appearing out of nowhere, hidden by the sun's glare, a sailboat was approaching the island.

It grew larger, and sailed up and down the shoreline as though inspecting the island, before turning at the crippled bell buoy and entering the harbor. Fearfully, John went down to the harbor shore with great curiosity. Skillfully the boat was anchored just off of the ruined dock and the captain came ashore in a dingy. It was a woman, who introduced herself as the daughter of the owner of the good ship *The Scorpion*, which was reported to have foundered near this island years ago. Midnight looked her over with fascination, a middle aged woman wearing salt-stained clothes.

She explained further that *The Scorpion* was a small wooden coastal freighter that her father had purchased and converted into a private luxury vessel which could be publicly chartered for special events. She continued. "My fathers' nickname as a scorpion was well earned. He believed in the simple message that all promises should be kept and all contracts honored. Like a scorpion, he would sting if he felt that he could not withdraw honorably from a situation that endangered him physically or diminished him monetarily."

Chapter 30
"A Message Came From My Father"

My father kept in touch with me.

He told me by radio that he hired a deckhand to help him run his boat, loading and unloading as my guests needed. The new hand was useful and experienced at sea and in port. The guests seemed to like him although he seemed to like to spend much time below decks in the holds. The male guest was a wonderful musician and spends much time practicing, his wonderful musical melodies carrying far from the boat, both while at sea or providing beautiful melodies that flowed around us when we were in port, delighting the nearby population of neighbors or citizens.

One night while we were all sleeping the deckhand was discovered prowling in the storage quarters of our guests, helping himself to small items at first, and then stealthily discovering ways to enter the more secure storage compartments of the boat. Our guests explained their fears to me, although they had kept a very private secret of the material that they had brought aboard and had given me very few details of the purpose of their cruise. They paid me well for the privilege of use of *The Scorpion* and that is all that was asked of them.

However, the deckhand was closely watched and one day when we grew close to land, knowing I suspected him as a thief, he tried to kill me and throw me overboard. When the fight broke out we both were armed and ready, I was at the stern of the boat, trying to secure the lashing of the dingy that allowed us to go ashore once we were anchored. Emerging from the hold at mid-ship he took several quick shots at me. The first missed and I tried to duck out of sight. The second shot nicked me in my shoulder, but it was not the hand which held my own gun, He didn't realize that he had hit me and he ran forward towards the bow, trying to find a place to hide, lest I shoot back, which I did, several times. With the boat rocking in the waves my shots were not very accurate. I almost emptied my gun and I was down to my last bullet when I steadied myself as best I could and fired again.

His running stopped and he fell to the deck, his right leg collapsing beneath him, a stream of blood flowing from his knee, the projectile having smashed his kneecap and found its way though the flesh and bone, leaving his leg unable to bear his weight, he fell to the deck, and in great pain staggered to his feet and then with the next crashing wave, lost his balance and fell overboard.

The evening light faded into darkness. I was tempted to call "Man overboard!" but there was no one capable of rescuing him. The boat hit the bottom and slammed into the sand. It turned sideways, and then was driven higher and higher onto the beach. I called out, "Abandon Ship!" With the great breaking waves pounding against our hull

Our guests struggled against the violent movement of the boat as they climbed out of the holds to our upper deck, leaving the compartments below where they had been securing their musical instruments, artwork, and other personal property for fear of it being broken to pieces or washed overboard and left far up into the dunes. Soon, before they could put on any survival gear they too were washed overboard and never seen again, disappearing in the foam and froth.

Alone, I went below. The sea had begun to strip everything from the superstructure of the deck and with my injured shoulder I could barely hang on. With growing pain in my shoulder I retreated down to my small cabin in the most forward part of my boat, "The Scorpion." and watched the seawater seeping into the hull. There was barely enough charge left in my boat's radio to send this message to my daughter, giving her my location and circumstances. There was no answer.

This is what happened between me and my crewmember. I had hired an unknown, but skilled deck hand and taken aboard a charter party of two people, a wealthy musician and his beautiful artist wife who wished to make a special visit to a remote island.

Ready to sail and unknown to me, the couple had filled the hold of the Scorpion with a stolen treasure of gold coins and jewels which they were smuggling out of the country. After beginning their voyage, as they passed along the shoreline of Howling Head, the new deck hand of *The Scorpion* had discovered the treasure and decided to hijack my boat. We struggled for control and both were both shot as the boat approached Howling Head. The crew man was wounded and I saw him go overboard. I then radioed my position to my daughter and described my own condition as probably being fatally injured. Bleeding profusely,

I returned to my bunk in the forward cabin as the weather grew worse. The unmanned boat began to wallow in the high seas and soon drifted upon the beaches of Howling Head. The two frightened guests decided to abandon the ship, launching the lifeboat as best they could. In their inexperienced hands the ship was swamped almost immediately and they were never seen again. The hull of *The Scorpion*, minus its superstructure which was torn away, was carried high upon the deserted beach and upright was hidden among the dunes by drifting sands and brush.

John remembered the hull, though this was the first time that he was sure that it was not just a hallucination brought on by drinking the contents of the strange black bottles. If his memory of the old hull was true and it really did exist, then maybe his other dreams were also true. Maybe Hannah still was alive. He described to the woman the ship and its contents and she was overjoyed at the accuracy of his description.

"Where is it now?" she asked.

"I don't know, it washed away some time ago, but it may still be near, sunken somewhere on the bottom in the quiet water in the back of the harbor. We will begin to look for it when you are ready.

And so they did. They found the hull sitting upright on the bottom in a secluded portion of the harbor, weighted down by the treasure, in a place with little current that would muddy the water. The Scorpion's Daughter dove onto the wreck, and surely enough, found the treasure intact, and after prying the door of the tiny front cabin open, her father's bones, sitting upright on his bunk in the bow of the boat, stared back at her. She returned to the surface and retrieved an urn from her cabin.

When I spoke to the Scorpion's daughter and asked her why the treasure that I had salvaged from the abandoned hull of her father's ship, *The Scorpion*, and then carried to Whale Island was not the treasure of gold and jewels that I believed it to be, she replied: "Neither my father nor his guests were certain about the security of his boat and the crewman. Arrangements were made at an extra cost to have the flooring of that section of the hold temporarily removed and their real treasure stored secretly beneath it, almost as ballast. The old deck planking was then reinstalled and the sealed containers of shells and pebbles were then place on top again in the dim hold."

"Why did I believe the shells and pebbles were gold and jewels?" I asked. "Maybe it was exhaustion, hunger, loneliness or drinking too much of the contents of the dark bottles." The Scorpion's daughter continued, "In any event, the secret hiding place worked well, fortunately I knew it and now the treasure has been rescued. I will give you a fair share in return for your help finding my father's wrecked boat and recovering the treasure." I thanked her and planned to see my lover Hannah again with the gift of great value.

"I came to find the remains of *The Scorpion* and of my father's body, too, if that was possible after all of these years. This area of the coast, with the bell buoy and the canine shaped islet, was described to me by him as he was dying. I promised him that I would come for him." Holding up a beautiful ceramic urn she said, "These are my mother's ashes. She died of a broken heart when she learned that he had been lost at sea. I promised her that I would find him and reunite them. I am going to do that now and leave her ashes with his body. When this promise is fulfilled I will remove any of the treasure that remains in the hull and take it with me to a secret place that my father recommended."

So saying, she dove below into the still, clear water of the lagoon, making her way below deck into the forward compartment and opening the cabin door. Her fathers' bones rested intact still wearing his captain's cap. She placed the urn in the bones of his arms and carefully closed the door. Returning to the surface she said to John "I have kept my promise to my mother and father. They are reunited, as they wished to be. Let's gather the remaining treasure from the hold and I will take it to its new home as he would want me to do." Thank you for your help. You are entitled to a fair share.

And so, one bucket at a time, we pulled the shining riches to the surface and poured them into the hold of *The Scorpion's Widow*. When *The Scorpion* was empty, she told me that she would take me to Whale Island and leave me there on her way to her own secret destination, leaving me there to be with my beautiful Hannah. She would then give Hannah and me a chest of gold and jewels as a wedding present, the treasures that I had already taken were an extra gift for my help in finding *The Scorpion's* resting place on the bottom of the bay.

John Kettle was stunned that this mysterious woman would know so much about him, but even more excited to know that Hannah and Whale Island were not just a dream. She explained to him, that in her search for her father's sunken vessel she had stopped at Whale Island to seek more information about the wreck and had been told of John Kettle's strange disappearance from that place immediately after the wedding. They sailed together to Whale Island.

After a joyful reuniting anchorage in that harbor, after re-supplying the boat with all of its needs, a pair of great whales, one on either side of the boat, guided the newly named *The Scorpion's Daughter* through the narrow mouth of the safe harbor and out to the open sea until it met a favorable wind. The Scorpion's daughter raised the sail and began her voyage. A school of porpoises leaped from the water, circling around the boat to the great amusement of John and Hannah and their citizens who were watching from the shore. Midnight flew to the top of the white castle and "cawed" out an excited farewell. The Scorpion's daughter sailed away in peace to a destination known only to her.

It is quiet again on Howling Head Island. The trees and the vines and the brush, having overgrown most of the town, have crushed the remains of the humble buildings which once flourished there. The barely discernible Long Boat Inn and the village road are disappearing. The pilings of the wharfs have been tilted, battered and lifted by the winter ice. The fields and orchards have reverted back to forest. Circling crows search the trees below for the hidden owls, which in turn hunt for crows and small animals in the darkness. Hungry gulls still wait for the bounty of the sea to be delivered onto the lonely beaches. When the fierce winds blow from the sea, the tormented bell buoy still clangs, singing a strange duet with the wolf-like calls from the islet of Howling Head Island.

John Kettle, with his companion, the black crow "Midnight" on his shoulder, Midnight wearing the familiar brass bell around his neck that rings a little every time he moves, sit in the great white castle overlooking the harbor. The beautiful Queen Hannah, healed from her scars, sits by their side, ruling in peace and joy while overlooking the sea on the sunny hill of Whale Island. All is well.

Chapter 31

A Final Departure

A new boat, named *The Scorpion's Daughter,* and skippered by its namesake, prepared for a journey to a destination known only to her, guided by charts drawn only for her and by her father. The boat's hull filled with the treasure that the previous occupants had gathered. Needing some physical help on the boat to complete the mysterious voyage the Scorpion's daughter hired a limping old man who had lived almost as a beggar on Whale island, and who claimed that he would be more than glad to have a paying job as well as a bunk to sleep in after so long living in poverty around the wharfs of Whale Island.

A quiet group of inhabitants gathered at the harbor to wish The Scorpion's daughter good luck on her adventure, though she gave no information to anyone regarding her destination. John Kettle and his Queen Hannah bid her well and supplied the boat with supplies that filled its galley and fuel tanks. A school of glistening whales gathered just outside of the harbor to escort the boat out into the open sea, away from Whale Island, until favorable winds provided a quick start to the voyage. All went well for the first several days, clear skies, favorable breezes and a calm sea.

One misty night the captain left the hired crewman at the wheel while she caught some sleep. She was awakened by the sound of her cabin door being opened and without showing that she was awake she watched through almost closed eyes

The Last Man On Howling Head Island

as the crewman went below on muffled feet and brought up small bags of treasure, taking them outside and then back to the small boat towed behind the larger vessel, where he hid them under the seats. The captain had also hidden many precious jewels and coins at the bottom of a large cylindrical metal container that hung on her cabin wall. She had it labeled as "Charts," the maps of the sea, which were used in the navigation of the open sea to keep the boat going in the right direction. The stealthy crewman quietly took the Chart Box off of the wall, glancing at her to make sure that she was still asleep and took it outside and then went back and climbed into to the dingy. He opened the chart box there and reached down inside of it to examine the beautiful diamonds and rubies and to count the glistening gold coins.

Unknown to him, as a favor to her father's memory, she had kept a cage full of his favorite pets aboard the new ship, (some huge scorpions), and dropped several of them into the chart box as a security factor. The crewman in the dingy now reached down to the bottom of the box to examine the riches and was severely stung as he grasped the treasure that was full of scorpions. His hands immediately were stung and his fingers lost feeling. He tried to pull the dingy back to the transom of the parent ship, but could not grasp the line. Looking up, he saw the Scorpion's daughter looking down at him, a glass bottle of gasoline in her hands with a length of cloth stuffed in its neck. Rushing to the bow of his little craft he tried to release the line that bound the two crafts together. His hands remained swollen and without feeling and there was nothing that he could do to escape. He screamed at the woman! "Oh, Scorpion's Daughter, I am sorry about the death of your father. I didn't intend to rob and kill him, or harm his guests. All they had to do was go ashore by themselves and turn the boat over to me. I could have sailed away to my own secret safe place and they could have all been safe on Howling Head Island."

The Scorpion's daughter, said nothing, but produced a match from her pocket and lit the wick of her glass bomb. The man in the dingy tried to climb overboard but now the poison was affecting his arms and legs and he was helpless. She lofted the burning bomb into the small craft which immediately blew up, scattering all that it contained into the quiet sea. When the flames burned out the only thing that remained bobbing on the surface was the metal chart box. The Scorpion's daughter maneuvered her boat through the small amount of other debris until she was able to retrieve the Chart Box and hang it again on its holder on the bulkhead of her cabin.

As darkness fell, drifting over the waves, there came the faint sound of a distant bell buoy, softly clanging somewhere in a distant unknown harbor. There was also an indistinct glimmer of a blinking light which might have been a star, or a buoy, floating low on the horizon. On the next beautiful morning the Scorpion's daughter, now well rested, continued her voyage, escorted again by six small whales that appeared out of nowhere to guide her. Flitting around the top of her mast were three Purple Starred Butterflies, endlessly dropping a glistening golden powder over the mast, the rigging, the deck below and the occupant resting in the cabin of her boat below. All was good in the world.

On Whale Island, John Kettle, with Midnight the crow on his shoulder and Hannah the Queen next to him watched as the six whales happily returned to the safe harbor. Knowing that all was well John and Hannah returned to the palace and were content and happy for the rest of their lives.

Midnight rustled his feathers and the gleaming bell around his neck rang joyously.